W9-BNR-963

THE SHORTEST DAY

MURDER AT THE REVELS

◇　　◇　　◇　　◇

A Homer Kelly Mystery

VIKING
Mystery
Suspense

THE
SHORTEST DAY

MURDER AT THE REVELS

A Homer Kelly Mystery

ILLUSTRATIONS BY THE AUTHOR

Jane Langton

VIKING

VIKING
Published by the Penguin Group
Penguin Books USA Inc., 375 Hudson Street, New York, New York 10014, U.S.A.
Penguin Books Ltd, 27 Wrights Lane, London W8 5TZ, England
Penguin Books Australia Ltd, Ringwood, Victoria, Australia
Penguin Books Canada Ltd, 10 Alcorn Avenue, Toronto, Ontario, Canada M4V 3B2
Penguin Books (N.Z.) Ltd, 182–190 Wairau Road, Auckland 10, New Zealand

Penguin Books Ltd, Registered Offices:
Harmondsworth, Middlesex, England

First published in 1995 by Viking Penguin,
a division of Penguin Books USA Inc.

1   3   5   7   9   10   8   6   4   2

PUBLISHER'S NOTE

This is a work of fiction. Names, characters, places, and incidents either are the product of the author's imagination or are used fictitiously, and any resemblance to actual persons, living or dead, events, or locales is entirely coincidental.

Many of the verses used as epigraphs in this book are taken from songs and carols in *The Christmas Revels Songbook*, compiled by Nancy and John Langstaff (David R. Godine, 1985). Excerpts from John Langstaff's mummer's play, *Saint George and the Dragon* (Atheneum, 1973), appear as some of the lines spoken by fictional characters acting as mummers and as a number of epigraphs and are used with his permission. An excerpt from Susan Cooper's poem, "The Shortest Day," passages from her dramatized version of *Sir Gawain and the Green Knight*, and her words to the carol "Sing We Noel" and the song "Orientis Partibus" are used with her permission. Verse from "Love Is Come Again" ("Now the green blade riseth . . ."), words by J. M. C. Crum, from *The Oxford Book of Carols*. © Oxford University Press 1928. Used by permission of Oxford University Press.

Library of Congress Cataloging-in-Publication Data
Langton, Jane.
The shortest day: murder at the revels / Jane Langton.
p.   cm.
ISBN 0-670-84710-0
1. Kelly, Homer (Fictitious character)—Fiction.
2. Massachusetts—Fiction.   I. Title.
PS3562.A515S56   1995
813'.54—dc20   95-14266

This book is printed on acid-free paper.

Printed in the United States of America
Set in Stempel Schneidler
Designed by Ann Gold

FOR STEWART GUERNSEY

So the shortest day came,
and the year died,
And everywhere down the centuries
of the snow-white world
Came people singing, dancing,
To drive the dark away....

Susan Cooper

◇ ◇ ◇ ◇ ◇ ◇ ◇ ◇ ◇ ◇ ◇ ◇

PART ONE

THE CALL FOR ROOM

Room, room, brave gallants all!
Pray give us room to rhyme!
We've come to show activity upon this wintertime.
Activity of youth, activity of age,
Such activity as you've never seen on stage!

Saint George and the Dragon

◇ ◇ ◇ ◇ ◇ ◇ ◇ ◇ ◇ ◇ ◇ ◇

CHAPTER 1

O I shall be as dead, mother,
As stones are in the wall;
O the stones in the streets, mother,
Shall sorrow for me all.
        "The Cherry Tree Carol"

The death of the folk singer from the South was a bitter disappointment to everyone who had bought tickets for the Christmas Revels. Last year, in every performance, he had captivated the audience in Memorial Hall. Middle-aged women were crazy about him. Already this year several women students from the Harvard Business School and another from the Law School had tried to date Henry Shady, even though he had only a fourth-grade education, having spent most of his life excavating bituminous coal in Filbert, West Virginia.

Mary Kelly was a witness to the accident, or almost a witness. She heard the sound of the approaching car and then the thud and the squeal of brakes. But her back was turned. She was climbing the steps of Memorial Hall on her way to a Revels rehearsal. She whirled around and saw the big Range Rover heave backward and thump down off the body. As the driver burst out of the car she ran down the steps, and both of them bent over the poor kid with the crushed skull.

It was apparent that he was beyond help. At once Mary recognized the crude country haircut and cheap overcoat

3

belonging to Henry Shady. Sickened with pity, she stood up, then staggered back as the demented driver fell on her, sobbing, and clung to her, choking out the same words over and over, "He ran in front of me. I couldn't stop, I couldn't stop."

A crowd was gathering. Revels people on their way to the evening rehearsal stopped to see what was going on and gasped in stunned recognition. "Oh, my God, it's Henry."

"Who?"

"Henry Shady."

"Oh, no, not Henry Shady."

Mary was still caught in the grip of the sobbing driver. "Look," she said, trying to speak over his shoulder, "would someone—please call the police? There's a phone—inside the door."

And then all the rest of the Revels people poured out the north door of Memorial Hall and stood in a shocked ring around the body of Henry Shady. A flashlight flickered over his ruined face, someone said "Don't," and the light vanished. There was the sound of weeping.

Mary was frozen in a grim geometrical tableau—she and the driver were a clumsy vertical, Henry Shady was the horizontal, the onlookers were an enclosing circle. Would the police never come? Then the driver loosened his hold on her neck and cried, "Sarah," and the circle opened to let someone through. "I'm sorry, Sarah," gasped the driver. "I'm sorry, I'm sorry."

Sarah Bailey cast one look down at Henry Shady, then reached out her arms to the man whose car had run over him. They stood together in the hush, clinging to each other, rocking a little back and forth, Sarah murmuring like a mother comforting a child.

Oh, God, how terrible, thought Mary. The poor heartbroken driver must be Morgan Bailey, Sarah's husband. Sarah was the director of all that was going on in Memorial Hall's Sanders Theatre; she had discovered Henry Shady in the first place, and invited him northward last year, and made him once again the ornament of this year's Revels. And now it was Sarah's own husband who had killed him! No wonder the poor guy kept sobbing and protesting that it wasn't his fault. "I couldn't help it, Sarah. I'm sorry, I'm so sorry."

Thank God, the police cruiser was pulling up at last, followed by an ambulance with its lights flashing.

The police took the names of witnesses—only one in this case, Mary Kelly. "And I wasn't really a witness," said Mary. "I mean, I didn't really see it when it happened. I just heard the squeal of brakes and the noise of the impact. No"—Mary corrected herself—"the impact and the squeal of the brakes."

The officer did not notice the distinction. He asked a few questions of Morgan Bailey, then bundled him into the cruiser with Sarah and drove away, as the body of Henry Shady disappeared in the back of the ambulance.

The slam of the ambulance door was a note of finality. The circle of onlookers drifted away, whispering, consoling one another, crying a little.

One of them was Arlo Field. Arlo was supposed to be taking the part of Saint George in the Revels, but he didn't know if he could handle it or not. He had been thinking of backing out. He was a scientist, not one of your artsyfartsy kinds of people.

But now he changed his mind. Sarah had enough troubles. He couldn't give her one more. Silently he turned away, and then someone touched his arm.

It was one of the Morris dancers. "Tom says, come back on Friday at the same time. Okay?"

"Okay," murmured Arlo. "I'll be there."

In the Cambridge Police Headquarters, on Western Avenue, the sergeant interviewing Morgan Bailey abandoned the severity he usually assumed in handling careless drivers— this one seemed so inconsolable, so tortured by shame and sorrow. Instead of condemning Morgan, Sergeant Hasty did his best to comfort him.

"It looks to me like an accident, pure and simple. I mean, there was no liquor involved. You've got a clean driving record. But the poor guy's family may want to press charges. I suggest you hire a lawyer."

Sarah Bailey thanked him. Morgan tried to thank him, but he was still almost unable to speak.

Sergeant Hasty reached over to pat his arm. "Have you got a pastor? That would be the best thing. Talk to your priest, or, you know, your minister. Whatever."

As it turned out, no action was taken against Morgan Bailey. No one pressed charges. Henry Shady's mother, down there in Filbert, West Virginia, was prostrated when the local police called her with the news that her youngest son had been killed in a traffic accident in Cambridge, Massachusetts, but it never occurred to her to sue. Mrs. Shady was a simple hill woman. She didn't have the city sophistication to think in terms of million-dollar litigation. The splendor and might of civilized law practice, the stylized grandeur of suit and countersuit among the prosperous law firms of Boston's State Street, were entirely out of her ken. Heartsore, she knew only that she would never see her son again.

CHAPTER 2

O mortal man, remember well,
When Christ died on the rood,
'Twas for our sins and wicked ways
Christ shed his precious blood. . . .
                    "Sussex Mummers' Carol"

After explaining to the police what she had seen of the accident that killed Henry Shady and what she had not seen, Mary Kelly walked across the Yard to Harvard Square, took the T to the Alewife parking garage, extracted her car, and drove home to Concord to tell the news to her husband, Homer.

"Christ," he said, "the poor kid. I remember him from last year. Big young guy, sort of graceful, with a really nice voice? Too bad." Homer had been making himself a lonely dinner of scrambled eggs and onions. Now he took the pan off the fire and dumped in a couple more eggs.

Mary slumped into a kitchen chair and put her head in her hands. "You know, there were two or three funny things. I've been thinking about them on the way home."

"Funny things?"

"Oh, you know, strange. Why was this guy's big Range Rover up on the sidewalk? You'd think he would have been driving straight along Kirkland Street when poor Henry suddenly appeared out of the darkness, and then, wham, he would have run into him, so the car would still be right there on the street."

Homer swirled the eggs in the pan with a big spoon. "Did anybody ask him about that?"

"Oh, yes. He said he swerved up over the curb to try to

avoid the pedestrian, but the guy dodged the wrong way, so he couldn't help running into him."

Homer held his big spoon in the air and tried to picture the swerving car, the victim trying to jump out of the way, the fatal mistake. "Sounds plausible, I guess."

"I know, it sounds all right, but it's hard to see it happening. Homer, the eggs!"

Smoke poured from the frying pan. Homer yanked it off the fire and tried to stir the blackened mass of eggs and onions. They reeked of burning. "Goddamnit," he said, "it's your fault for distracting the master chef with your horrible stories."

"Here, Homer, let me do it." Mary took out another pan and found an onion in the basket under the counter.

"Well, go ahead, what else was there?" said Homer grumpily, backing out of the way.

"What else?"

"You said there were two or three funny things."

"Oh, right. Another thing was the order of events. I mean, hearing the accident with my back turned, I think the thud came first and then the squeal of brakes. You'd think it would be the other way around. You know, the squeal of brakes and then the sound of the impact." Mary turned and looked anxiously at her husband. "Wouldn't you, Homer?"

Homer laughed. "Listen, my darling, who is it around here who's always being blamed for acting like the lieutenant detective he used to be instead of a nice respectable teacher at an ancient institution of higher learning? Me, that's who. And now here you go, probing and prying and drawing crazy conclusions on no evidence at all. Forget it. It's bad enough, that poor kid coming up from the country to nasty old Massachusetts to be slaughtered on the street by some overeducated Ph.D. Let it go. After all, you're a nice respectable teacher at the same institution. It's none of your business."

"Right," said Mary, slamming down the frying pan. "I'll just tie on my apron and stay home and make my husband's supper."

"Well, excuse *me*."

"Oh, shut up, Homer, just shut up."

In the fuming atmosphere of the smoky kitchen and the emotional backwash of the tragic scene she had witnessed, Mary forgot the third thing until early the next morning. Then, lying in bed, staring at the ceiling and regretting the darkness of early December, she remembered how good it had been to wake up in the same room only two months ago. On an October dawn the bedroom would be flooded with autumn sunlight, and often a squadron of noisy migrating geese flew over the house to land on the river.

Mary sat up and poked Homer. "Listen, there was a third thing."

"Whumph?" Homer rolled over the other way and pulled the covers over his head.

"That accident yesterday, there was another odd thing about it." Mary lay down again and wrapped her arm around Homer. "I heard a bird go over, squawking."

Homer burrowed deeper into his pillow and muttered sleepily, "A bird?"

"I swear it sounded like wild geese flying over the river. I mean, you wouldn't think there'd be geese in Cambridge, would you, Homer? Right now, in the darkest days of the year?"

CHAPTER 3

When Joseph was an old man,
An old man was he,
He courted Virgin Mary,
The Queen of Galilee,
He courted Virgin Mary,
The Queen of Galilee.

As Joseph and Mary
Were in an orchard good,
There were apples, there were cherries,
As red as any blood,
There were apples, there were cherries,
As red as any blood.

Then Mary spoke to Joseph,
So meek and so mild,
"Joseph, gather me some cherries,
For I am with child.
Joseph, gather me some cherries,
For I am with child."

Then Joseph flew in anger,
In anger flew he,
"Let the father of the baby
Gather cherries for thee,
Let the father of the baby
Gather cherries for thee" . . .

"The Cherry Tree Carol"

It was a crisis. Henry Shady's death was a terrible
shame, but there was no time to mourn. The hole in
the program for this year's Revels had to be filled.

Sarah Bailey and Tom Cobb sat on one of the benches
at the front of the mezzanine in Sanders Theatre, staring at the stage. Around Sanders all the immense volumes

and compartmented spaces in Memorial Hall were empty.
Sarah and Tom were alone in the building.

The bare stage was unlit. The marble figures of James
Otis and Josiah Quincy gleamed pale at either side, but
there was no life in their changeless gestures. Otis clutched
a marble document labeled STAMP ACT, Quincy handed
a diploma to no one in particular. The gold-and-scarlet
Harvard shields praising VERITAS at the back of the stage
glowed only dimly, and the carved wooden faces of the
bears and foxes above the stage were noncommittal. It
hardly seemed possible that a horde of dancers and singers
would soon be capering and singing all over the dusty
wooden stage, while a host of fiddlers fiddled and a crowd
of pipers piped and seven trumpeters tooted their glitter-
ing horns, to fill the hall with the promised profusion of
Christmas merriment.

Of course, it wasn't just the festival of Christmas they
would be celebrating, it was also the winter solstice. Some
of the Revels themes had nothing to do with the birth of
Jesus. They were pagan stories, they were magic, they
were ancient rites challenging the cold of winter in its
darkest time, awakening the growth and greenness of the
spring. And some were wassails praising the joys of good
brown ale, and some were haunting entreaties to the wild
deer in the forest, appeals by the hunters to the hunted to
allow themselves to be killed. And always there was the
stamping and leaping of the Morris dancers, which had no
connection with the Christian nativity at all.

But this year it wasn't enough. Tom Cobb was alarmed.
What if they had to cancel the whole thing? If the program
fell apart, there would be no Revels this year, no celebration of Christmas or the solstice or brown ale or the hunt-
ing of the deer, no Morris dancing. The death of Henry

Shady had upset the entire schedule of dances, carols, choruses, children's songs and games, and the whole cluster of episodes centering around the story of Saint George.

Tom looked sideways at Sarah, his codirector. After Shady's death, how was she holding up? Sarah had been a sort of foster mother to Shady; in fact, you couldn't help wondering if she had been something even warmer and closer. And Henry had worshipped her, anybody could have seen that.

She seemed all right. But, poor Sarah, she must be walking an emotional tightrope. On the one hand she needed to grieve for Shady, but at the same time she had to comfort her fool of a husband, who had run over the poor kid from West Virginia. Her eyes were red, as though she had wept her share of tears, but otherwise she seemed like herself. Thank God, because there was nobody else who could fill her shoes.

Tom assessed the matter shrewdly. It was true, no one else in the entire Revels company could manage the annual production of the Christmas Revels with anything like Sarah's high-spirited competence and good judgment, certainly not Tom Cobb, her codirector. Of course, there was always Walter Shattuck, the Old Master, but Walt was no longer interested in running things. He was called the Old Master because he had founded the Revels in the first place, but he wasn't really old at all, and he had long since stopped acting as general manager. Now his only contribution to the annual celebration was his captivating voice—but that was a great contribution indeed. No one, not even the charismatic young folk singer from West Virginia, could sing like Walt. Now that Henry Shady was dead, they would surely have to fall back on Walt's spellbinding baritone to fatten their diminished program.

They had to decide. They had to choose something, and choose it right now—a whole chunk of guaranteed surefire Revels sorcery.

"We could always do 'The Cherry Tree Carol' again," said Sarah.

"Oh, God, Sarah, we've done it so often before." Tom broke a chocolate bar in two and offered her a piece.

Sarah took it hungrily. "But everybody loves 'The Cherry Tree Carol.' We've got the costumes. We've got that girl who took the part of Mary last year, and the guy who does the tree with the cherries growing out of his fingers, and we've got Walt to sing the song. And what about you? The way you took the part of Joseph was so perfect."

"You mean the way I stamped my feet in jealous rage?"

Sarah laughed. "Well, yes, I guess so. Mmmm, this is delicious. What do you call these things?"

"Tastychox. My favorite. Want some more? Well, listen, it's all right with me if we do 'The Cherry Tree' again. I'd forgotten about the jealous rage. That's why people like it so much. Everybody's jealous now and then, right?"

Sarah got up and stared at one of the east windows above the rows of mezzanine seats. It was glimmering faintly in the vanishing twilight, flashing now and then with the headlights of cars moving slowly along Cambridge Street. That way lay Inman Square and her apartment on Maple Avenue, where Morgan was waiting for her, getting supper, still suffering from what had happened yesterday. "You're right. Everybody's jealous now and then."

CHAPTER 4

Stir up the fire and make a light
And see our noble act tonight.
Traditional British Mummers' Play

The days were shriveling toward the shortest of the year, as the sun groped its way around the wintry end of its trajectory. But in Harvard Yard at four-thirty in the afternoon of the Friday after the accident that killed the folk singer from West Virginia, the sky was still bright. A crescent moon like a delicate ship rode low above the skyline, jibing in the cold squall that shook the tops of the trees.

But the Yard itself was deep in shadow. Here the air was amber, clotted with the insect bodies of dead professors—Mathers and Wares, a Lowell, a Channing, a Longfellow—all mashed wings and tangled jointed legs like flies. Through the leafless branches of the trees ten thousand particles of paper sifted down, worn off the edges of pages riffled by scholars' fingers in libraries and labs and offices scattered throughout the university. The dust swirled now in descending spirals in the light wind and drifted downward, falling in invisible granules on the cold cheeks of men and women passing to and fro.

Just north of the Yard, on the overpass above Cambridge Street, there was more glare and light. The setting sun glittered on the glass rooftops of the Science Center. Diagonally across the street the billion bricks of Memorial Hall massed themselves under a striped roof giddy with rosy color.

Homer Kelly had been teaching in Memorial Hall. All

day long it had seemed to him like an ordinary day. No memorial wreath lay on the north steps deploring the death of Henry Shady. No black crepe was tacked over the door. The only memorials in all the vast spaces of the building were the marble tablets in the high corridor recording the names of the men of Harvard who had fallen in the battles of Gettysburg, Wilderness, Antietam, Bull Run.

The lecture hall where Homer taught a course in American literature with his wife, Mary, was an ugly auditorium at the west end. On his way out, hauling on his gloves and holding a sheaf of papers in his teeth, he ran into the homeless old black man who often huddled out of the wind on the steps of the ground-floor entry. As usual he was swaddled in a blanket, his head down, his face invisible.

Homer dropped a quarter in front of him, as he always did, and murmured, "Good evening."

There was no response. The quarter lay where it had fallen. But after Homer was gone the old man's hand crept out of the blanket and grasped the coin. Then, like a mummy rising from a sarcophagus, he shambled to his feet.

Mary Kelly saw him a little while later as she climbed out of the subway at Church Street, emerging into the cold air of Harvard Square.

She looked around as she always did, savoring once again the zest and bite of the Square. The same tangle of streets had existed at this intersection since the seventeenth century. It was a crossroads for scholars of every stripe, and for students who had muscled their way through secondary school to enter Harvard's narrow portals, and for the thousands of Harvard employees who shuffled paper and kept the buildings going, and for high-school kids high-shouldered in Raiders jackets laughing loudly around the public phones, and for bicycle cultists riding too fast through the flow on the sidewalk. Between the BayBank and the Harvard Coop, the Peruvian band blew into its panpipes, *chuff-chuffa-chuff.*

Across the street the brick buildings and wrought-iron gates of Harvard Yard were the frontier to another world, but here in the Square the two worlds nudged each other and overlapped, and the flow went both ways, in and out.

DON'T WALK, said the light. Mary waited, fumbling in her purse for a coin to give the old black man who was settling down beside the subway entrance. He was often there, swathed in a blanket, paying no attention to the passersby. Today his hand emerged from the blanket to take Mary's quarter, then slid back inside. He did not look up.

WALK, said the light. Mary moved forward, stepping out onto Massachusetts Avenue in front of the growling cars. Then she glanced back. Someone was yelling, making a disturbance—*tent city for the homeless, come one, come all*—the words faded as he turned the other way—*put the screws on Harvard—moral responsibility—six-billion-dollar endowment!*

The voice was familiar. Mary stepped back on the pavement. Sure enough, it was Palmer Nifto, good old Palmer Nifto with a new list of nonnegotiable demands. A couple of years ago he had turned Mary's hometown of Concord on its ear, demanding housing for himself and his homeless friends, getting them all in trouble by breaking into a dwelling while its owners were away. Here he was again, making a public protest, trying to outshout a Cambridge policewoman who was yelling back at him, "Oh, for Christ's sake, Palmer, pipe down."

Mary grinned and crossed to the other side. She was supposed to be meeting Homer, and she was late. Poor Homer, he was being such a good sport. After supper he'd have to hang around all evening through her Revels rehearsal in order to join her on the T to Alewife to pick up her car, because his own was having transmission trouble. He'd be bored to death.

Mary hurried through the gate, tucking her mittened hands into her coat pockets. It was very cold in the Yard. Already, in early December, the frost had penetrated the ground. Its cold fingers had gone far down under the grassy turf to stiffen the soil. Worms no longer nosed blindly in and out and up and down. The larvae of Japanese beetles were curled in yellow coils, clasped by the frozen sod, waiting for spring. Now, at five o'clock, the sky was already dark. John Harvard was nearly invisible on his granite base, except for the snow on his bronze lap.

The thinnest curl of a moon hung over Massachusetts Hall, marking the place where the sun had gone down.

Mary waited at the bottom of the massive staircase of Widener Library, looking left and right for Homer, feeling guilty about the rehearsal. "You won't have to be involved at all," she had promised Homer. "I'll come and go to rehearsals and performances by myself. I really want to do this, Homer."

But here they were, welded together for the whole evening. Homer was going to loathe it. He hated the whole Revels idea, from first principles to the bells on the Morris men's knees. Morris dancers, he said, gave him a pain. So did ethnic costumes worn by descendants of the Pilgrim fathers and phony folk art created by employees of IBM and Smith-Barney. Adult men and women frisking around in costume—why didn't they grow up?

There he was, striding toward her along a path between patches of frozen grass. Mary looked at Homer critically as he came nearer, looking taller than ever in his long coat. His month-old beard looked terrible. She laughed. "Oh, Homer, when is it going to grow a little longer? It looks horrible."

"No, no," said Homer, "you don't understand. It's right in the forefront of fashion. La Mode Hobo. Haven't you heard? Where have you been? Don't you keep up? The style of the Great Depression, it's all the rage."

"Oh, Homer, you're making that up."

"No, I'm not, I swear. Look at those kids." Homer nodded at a couple of boys in greasy fedoras and ragged overcoats. Mary watched them trot down the vast staircase. They were discussing the theory of least squares, their coats dragging behind them.

She took Homer's arm. "Well, I don't care whether it's fashionable or not, your beard is at a really gruesome stage."

After supper they crossed the Yard again, and walked across the broad expanse of the mall above the sunken tunnel of Cambridge Street. A couple of homeless people had set up a crude shelter of wooden planks beside one of the hedges, and they were hammering it together, holding nails in their teeth.

Mary told Homer about Palmer Nifto. There he was in the square, still campaigning for homeless people, still being a thorn in somebody's side. "You know, Homer," she said, looking at the shapeless dwelling under construction, "I sometimes wonder how our ancestors survived the winter. How did they keep themselves alive?"

"Well," said Homer, making up a theory, "suppose you had a cow. You could bring it inside and snuggle up beside it. I doubt many people froze to death or starved."

Mary wasn't so sure. She looked back at the two men with their hammers. One of them was Palmer Nifto. They might have been peasants in Yugoslavia with the cold funneling down between the mountains, or Irish farmers with their potatoes going rotten, or frostbitten muzhiks on the Siberian steppes. How many thousands of people had not made it through the winter? How many winter perishings had there been since the beginning of time?

With their heads down against the wind, they scuttled along the south side of Memorial Hall, climbed the steps to the entry, and pulled open the heavy door.

CHAPTER 5

I open the door, I enter in.
I hope your favour we shall win.
Whether we stand or whether we fall,
We'll do our best to please you all.
    Traditional British Mummers' Play

G ratefully Mary and Homer entered the high corridor. A throng of muffled shapes crowded through
the door behind them, eager to get out of the
wind. Inside the building there was no wind, only a cold
breath moving down from the wooden vaults, sliding past
the marble tablets with their sad memorials, flowing
downward to creep past Mary's scarf and stiffen her freezing fingers. Somewhere in the lower reaches of Memorial
Hall there must surely be an enormous furnace, but no
gushes of steamy heat found their way into this lofty corridor. How many rich alumni and alumnae would it take to
install a dozen giant radiators among the memorials? Too
many, apparently.

"Come on, Homer. It'll be warmer in the great hall."

And it was. The furnace, from whatever dark hole it in-
habited, sent vast quantities of warm air on rising thermals
to the summit of the ceiling of the great hall, where giant
hammerbeams held up the roof. Downward currents
warmed the lower reaches of the gigantic room, where a
lot was going on. People were moving around in various
stages of undress. Long rows of tables stretched into the
distance, covered with props and costumes. There was an
undercurrent of laughter and good humor. Well, of course,
thought Mary, suppressing a feeling of bitterness, the

show must go on. Time in its heartless way had closed over the memory of Henry Shady, leaving no seam.

"My God," said Homer, goggling at the deer antlers, "what are those for?"

"The horn dance," said Mary. "It's really ancient. You'll see."

Homer looked up at the beams arching over the high rows of stained-glass windows, dark at this hour and color-less. Below the windows the drab walls were lined with portraits of Union generals and the busts of dead professors.

"I've always liked this place," he said, remember-ing a time of crisis, a chase up the balcony stairs. It had been one of those foolish occasions when Homer had been forced back into his long-defunct role as an ex–lieutenant detective in the office of the District Attorney of Middle-sex County. "What are they using this place for now? Sort of a giant dressing room?"

Mary introduced him to Tom Cobb, one of the stage directors, and Homer said, "How do you do," but a gaggle of children rushed past them in an endless stream, and Tom said, "Hey, wait for me," and took off after the children. Mary grasped Homer's arm and led him to a harried-looking woman hunched over an ironing board. "Our wardrobe supervisor, Joan Hill."

"I was just saying—" said Homer, but then a human cherry tree said, "Excuse me," and wobbled past them, heading for a mirror to inspect the twiggy growths growing out of its head. At once there was a clatter of small objects on the floor. "Shit," said the tree, "all my cherries fell off."

"Oh, God," said the wardrobe supervisor. She waved her iron at Mary, and at once the ironing board collapsed. "Oh, could you, dear? Would you? I've got to do some-thing about his cherries."

Mary picked up the ironing board. "Really, Homer, you don't have to stay. Why don't you go to a movie or something?"

"Don't be silly. I want to see what it's like."

"Well, just as you wish." Mary wet her finger and touched the iron. It hissed. Someone shouted for the Morris dancers.

"Oh, God," said Homer, "Morris dancers. All this folksy stuff, Ph.D.s and computer scientists pretending to be peasants. How do you stand it?"

"Oh, Homer, I knew you wouldn't like it." Mary drove the iron along a length of wrinkled cloth. "It's true, there's a kind of Cambridge chic about the Revels. But the Morris dancers are really great. Why don't you go into Sanders Theatre and watch?"

Grumpily Homer did as he was told. Once more he crossed the cold high corridor. After pushing through the swinging doors of Sanders, he was again in the warm air.

The place was already buzzing. Three people were hunched over the tech table at the back of the floor, their equipment on a board mounted over a couple of benches. Homer sat down nearby and folded his arms and looked grimly at the stage.

But he couldn't maintain his cynicism. As always, the hollow chamber captured him with its nineteenth-century air of varnished wooden comfort, with its shadowy stage and enclosing semicircle of seats in rising tiers. Somehow the place had a quasi-medieval feeling. It was a Gothico-Victorian hall in a forest of oak trees in which wild boar and leaping stags were hiding, with huntsmen dodging behind the railings of the mezzanine. Ulysses S. Grant would appear in a moment in the robes of King Arthur, and so would John Ruskin, masquerading as Sir Galahad.

Homer winced. Oh, God, here came the Morris men, clumping onstage.

"Not yet," shouted Tom Cobb. "Come on again. Wait for the music."

The Morris dancers clattered off. A guy with a concertina struck up a tiddly tune, and they tramped in a second time.

"Hold it," said Tom. "Wait for me." He jumped up on the stage and joined them as they began to dance.

Homer slumped back on the bench and scowled as the six men stamped their feet and clashed their sticks together. Then he sat up and stopped scowling. Grudgingly he admitted to himself that they were very good. *Thump* went the stamping feet, *crash* went the sticks.

The dance was finished. The Morris men stopped leaping up and down and looked at Tom uncertainly as he backed away to become a stage director again. "Okay, that's it, go off in procession." Then Tom raised his voice and shouted, "Chorus? You've got to come on as they go off. Chorus, where are you?"

They filed onstage from the left, ten men in tunics and long hose, ten women in bright gowns. Homer looked for Mary, but she was the last because she was the tallest. In spite of his disbelief in the whole thing, Homer beamed at his wife and shook his clasped hands over his head.

Mary turned to her neighbor and grinned artificially, pretending to be part of a jolly Christmas festival. At once there was an interruption. Tom Cobb said, "Wait, here's Sarah."

There was a hush. Everyone stared offstage as Sarah came breezing in, and then, to their embarrassment, her husband appeared behind her. Morgan Bailey was a stranger to Homer Kelly, but everyone else recognized Sarah's husband, the driver responsible for the death of her star performer, Henry Shady.

But the two Baileys were boldly grasping the nettle. Morgan followed Sarah up the steps to the stage and made a little speech about what had happened. His hours of weeping were over. His voice was clear, his words were sensible. "Of course the accident was my fault, but Henry appeared so suddenly, right in front of my car. I swerved to avoid him, but in trying to get out of my way he jumped in the same direction. Sarah has told me how much you all loved Henry Shady. I will bear the scar for the rest of my life."

Well, good for you, thought Homer, giving him credit.

Then Sarah talked about the fund they were organizing in Henry's memory, money to be collected for his family. "His mother," whispered one of the technicians to Homer, "down there in West Virginia."

There was loud applause from the Morris men and the members of the chorus, and from the technicians sitting beside Homer and the musicians clustered in the wings. Someone flourished a checkbook. Someone else tossed green bills in the air.

But of course it wasn't funny. Gravely Sarah Bailey waved her arm, urging the performers to carry on, and hurried down the steps again. Her husband followed. Then Morgan Bailey walked solemnly to the back of the hall and sat down by himself on a darkened bench, silhouetted against the light of the encircling aisle.

But Morgan wasn't really feeling solemn at all. Instead he was oddly exhilarated. It was so strange, after all that weeping and mortification, he had awakened yesterday morning feeling buoyant and lighthearted. A weight had been lifted from his chest. Smiling, Morgan filled his lungs with the glowing air of Sanders Theatre and held it a moment, then let it go.

Seventeen rows in front of Morgan Bailey, Homer Kelly glowered as the chorus began to sing. They were all pretending to frolic as if it were the jolliest party anybody ever saw—like a cocktail party on Fayerweather Street, thought Homer sardonically.

"Okay," shouted Sarah, "time for the boar's head. Boar's head, where are you?"

In spite of himself, Homer was charmed as four girls in bright tunics carried onstage a giant tray on which lay a huge papier-mâché boar's head in a nest of ivy. When the chorus struck up "The Boar's Head Carol," he couldn't help nodding his shaggy head in time to the music.

From then on Homer forgot his hostility and basked in this fanciful Cambridge version of the Middle Ages. It was nice, it was the *Très Riches Heures* come to life, enhanced by the mystic Victorian woodwork of Memorial Hall, with its thick varnish in which were magically embedded a few fragments of the Round Table. The playful enchantment of the Revels had taken hold.

When Mary's part of the rehearsal was over, she met Homer in the deathlike chill of the memorial corridor. "Oh, Homer, I was right. You didn't like it, did you?"

He was not yet ready to confess his transformation. "Well, I don't know," he said gruffly. "The Morris dancers were okay, I guess."

Mary introduced him to Sarah and Morgan Bailey. Sarah was enchanted with Homer. She gaped up at him. "So this is the famous Homer Kelly! Nobody told me you were ten feet tall."

"Only nine feet, actually," murmured Homer, who was used to being stared at, and liked it.

"No, no," said Mary. "He's only six feet six."

"Oh, Homer," pleaded Sarah, taking his arm, "will you be our giant? We were going to do without one, but you're just right. We've never had anybody so tall."

"Great idea," said Tom Cobb, grinning at Homer. "How about it?"

Homer demurred bashfully, and then, to Mary's astonishment, he grinned and gave in. "Well, what the hell, I have to be in this building all the time anyway to teach our class." He cleared his throat and roared, "FEE-FI-FO-FUM—is that the general idea?"

Sarah threw back her head and laughed. "Oh, Homer, that's great."

Homer looked pleased with himself, his entire attitude toward childish playacting and Christmas frivolity and grown men and women making fools of themselves suddenly abandoned.

Mary was amused. She glanced at Morgan, Sarah's husband, and laughed. Morgan was smiling too, but his eyes were on Sarah.

"Saint George," cried Sarah. "Has anyone seen Saint George?"

Homer looked at his wife and raised his eyebrows. "Saint George?"

"Oh, you know, Homer, Saint George has to kill the dragon. And then he has to be killed himself, you see."

"No, I don't see."

Before Mary could explain, an interpreter loomed up beside them, a gaunt woman in thick glasses. Her enormously magnified eyes gazed at Homer. She launched into a lecture. "Dying and reviving gods, you see. The hero combat. In remote times the kings of Babylon were put to death after reigning for a single year. It's the sacrifice of the god-king, you see, to save the world. Among the Musurongo of the Congo the king is put to death after only a single day."

Mary was struck dumb. She repeated stupidly, "The Musurongo of the Congo?" Then she pulled herself together. "How do you do? I'm Mary Kelly, and this is my husband, Homer."

"Marguerite Box. *Dr.* Marguerite Box. Lecturer in mythology and folklore, the safeguarding of the life-spirit, the forms of taboo, the emblems of fertility, the worship of Adonis, the slaying of the god-king, et cetera." Dr. Box wore a large purple hat. Briefcases hung from her shoulders like panniers on a beast of burden.

Homer's eyes glazed over. Dr. Box was a bore. She fixed him with her magnified eye. "The legend of Saint George is merely a winter-solstice festival to revive the light, a new incarnation of a dying and reviving God." Then a blast of chill air smote Dr. Box, and she snatched at her purple hat.

Parents were shepherding children out the north door. They were a wriggling crowd in puffy coats and woolly hats, screeching in the cold, blocking the entrance for someone on his way in. The newcomer was Arlo Field. He crushed himself against the doorjamb to let them go by.

Sarah Bailey hugged him and dragged him inside. "Oh, Arlo, here you are. Saint George in person, come to save us from the dragon."

Mary and Homer Kelly followed the children out, while Sarah tucked one arm into Saint George's and the other into Tom Cobb's and hurried them into Sanders Theatre, trailed by Dr. Box.

Morgan Bailey followed Dr. Box, asking himself, *Who is the dragon?*, answering grimly, *I am. I am the dragon.*

CHAPTER 6

Here come I, St George, I've many hazards run,
And fought in every land that lies beneath the sun.
I am a famous champion,
Likewise a worthy knight,
And from Britain did I spring
And will uphold her might.
                                    Traditional British Mummers' Play

Arlo's part of the rehearsal was over. He had put on the tunic of the Red Cross Knight, he had killed the comic dragon and been killed in turn by the swords of the Morris dancers. Then he had been brought back to life by the funny Doctor, and Sarah Bailey had hugged him again, and told him to come back tomorrow.

He was released. Opening the north door of the memorial corridor, he stepped out into the cold night air, looked up to see what the universe was doing, and set off for his office in the Science Center. As an assistant professor in the astronomy department, Arlo had the use of the laboratory on the eighth floor. That was his professional address—Room 804, Science Center, Oxford Street, Cambridge, Massachusetts 02138. His home address was in Cambridge too—Apartment B, 329 Huron Avenue.

It amused him sometimes to remember the way he had written his address as a twelve-year-old boy in Belmont, seventeen years ago—

Arlo Thomas Field
47 Orchard Street
Town of Belmont

County of Middlesex
Commonwealth of Massachusetts
New England
Atlantic Seaboard
United States of America
Continent of North America
Western Hemisphere
The Earth
The Solar System
The Milky Way Galaxy
The Universe

Some of his friends, clever snotty little kids like himself, had written their addresses like that too. Later on, Arlo had run across the same thing in a play by Thornton Wilder, the cosmic address of one of the protagonists, beginning with Grovers Corners, New Hampshire, and ending with

The Mind of God

At twelve, Arlo had been a strict atheist, and he had left out the mind of God. Now, as an adult, he didn't exactly believe in a Christian God, but he wasn't an atheist either. How could an astronomer be an atheist? How could he look at his photographs of solar flares in the light of the alpha line of hydrogen—immense magnetic explosions one hundred thousand kilometers across—or see X-ray images of coronal holes blotching the face of the sun, how could he examine the faint spectra of star systems on the remote edges of the visible universe—and not be some kind of mystic?

Most of the time Arlo didn't bother to think about it. He lived and walked and breathed in a giant globe of stars and galaxies and dark matter and interstellar dust, he was penetrated by neutrinos from the sun's core and cosmic rays from somewhere in deep space. It was the ground of his being.

Now, as he crossed the mall over Cambridge Street under a sky emptied of stars by the glare of the city, Arlo's upward gaze was rewarded by nothing but the starboard lights of a plane heading for Logan. The Science Center was a checkered pyramid of light. Beyond its glassy geometry the other buildings along Oxford Street were dark shapes, hard and crystalline, as if they might shatter in the cold. Arlo knew they housed a hundred branches of scientific study—in the Museum of Comparative Zoology, for example, there was an exhibit of blown-glass flowers and a spider collection and a stuffed pangolin with round glass eyes—but now the museum was only a chunk of frozen brick and stone.

The night was really freezing. The cold was no surprise, because the days were growing shorter as the Northern Hemisphere leaned away from the sun and raced into the shadow. Arlo hunched his shoulders and thrust his gloved hands into his pockets and warmed himself by thinking about Sarah Bailey. Her embraces were worth remembering. Sarah was all warmth and red cheeks, frowsy red hair, uncoordinated pieces of clothing, and pillowed surfaces. In Sarah a generous mother nature had created a messy masterpiece. Her affection was a congratulation from the center of the earth. Unfortunately, it didn't mean anything in particular. Sarah hugged everybody. Her wholesome regard for the entire human race radiated in all directions, landing on tables and chairs.

It was too bad. Arlo thought of the other women in his life, a couple of girlfriends with whom he had been violently in love at one time or another. They had been like fleshly gardens full of flowering promise, but just below the surface they had turned out to be rock, solid rock, like the granite ledges under his mother's lawn.

The first had been a pretty woman with the perfect features of her wealthy ancestors, people with their pick of eligible mates. Cindy had learned in prep school to rule nations and govern empires. Her voice was loud and commanding. Arlo guessed she would settle for running the Milton Academy phonathon and the capital drive for the Boston Museum of Fine Arts.

The second was classic New Age. Totty was all scented candles, aromatherapy, Tarot cards, and Birkenstocks. For his birthday she had given him a crystal to dangle over his arm. He couldn't make it work. "Look," Totty said, "see what happens when I do it." Suspended over her own arm, the crystal began at once to swing gently, then faster and faster. "You're making it do that," said Arlo. "No, no, I swear, it's my own subconscious energy. I'm not doing a thing."

Arlo the scientist had said, "What exactly do you mean by energy?" and Totty had talked about vibrations and auras and forces and pretty soon they were shouting at each other.

From these two, Arlo had learned to be wary of hockey trophies and loud voices, bangles, spacey music, and Indian sitars. Therefore he was cautious, perhaps too cautious. Probably he just didn't know how to talk to women.

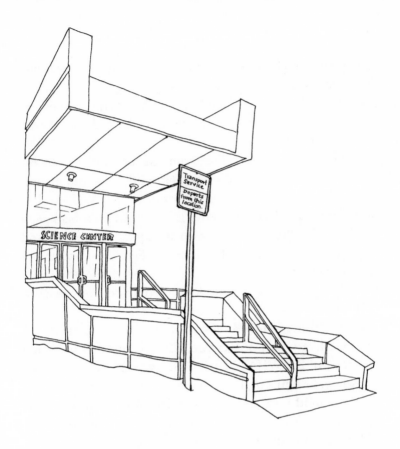

But with Sarah Bailey you wouldn't have to figure out how to talk. You could just be yourself. Well, it didn't matter. Sarah was unavailable, she was married. Naturally she was married. All the good ones were attached to somebody else. Arlo wondered what her husband was like when he wasn't committing manslaughter. Did he deserve a wife like Sarah?

Cautiously Arlo pushed open the door of the Science Center, hoping to avoid the old man who usually occupied the corner of the entry on cold nights. But Guthrie was there. Arlo flinched, and tried to hurry past him, but the old man stretched out his hand. "Hey, guy, I wanta tell you something, I wanta tell you something."

Arlo stopped and turned back. "What is it, Guthrie?" he said warily, remembering all the times he had been bored to death by Guthrie.

"Didn't you know? They run me off. I tell you, for what? For what? What did I do? Nothin'! They run me off! I didn't do nothin', and they run me off. For WHAT? Listen, I wanta tell you something." The old man beckoned to Arlo, then reached out with unexpected strength and pulled Arlo's face down to his own. "See, I just wanta tell you something."

"Well, what is it?" said Arlo. "What do you want to tell me?"

The old man smiled. His smile was saintly. "Listen, I mean, I like you, I *respect* you. I just wanta tell you they run me off! For WHAT? I ask you, for WHAT?"

Arlo gave him a dollar, and made a rush for the elevator, while behind him the old man tried to catch a couple of students bursting in from outside. As the elevator door closed, Arlo could see them ignoring him, hurrying past, staring straight ahead.

Arlo forgot Guthrie as the elevator rose to the eighth floor. He was eager to check on his camera. Time was growing short. The last exposures would have to be just right.

He found his graduate assistant in the astronomy lab, Chickie Pickett. "Hey, man," Arlo's colleague had said, after getting his first eyeful of Chickie, "how about sharing the goodies?" Because Chickie didn't look like the other women graduate assistants, who went around in athletic pants and heavy sneakers. Chickie wore bows in her hair and went in for four-inch heels and plunging necklines. She was upholstered in pearly gobbets of flesh. Chickie was writing a dissertation on the convection layer under the solar photosphere, but she looked like Betty Boop.

"Is everything okay?" said Arlo, tenderly inspecting his camera. It looked all right. It was still taped to the floor next to the big glass window, its lens pointing east to the sky above the roof of Memorial Hall.

"I was here this morning at eight-thirty," said Chickie, "and it opened and went click, right on the button. Only two more exposures, one a week from today and the last one on the shortest day." Chickie fluttered her eyelashes at Arlo. "Then you can take a look at your whole year's work. I can hardly wait. The analemma on film! Forty-four suns in one picture!"

"I hope to God nothing goes wrong. If the power goes down, the timing will be off. It could ruin everything."

"Or what if somebody joggles the camera? That Professor Finch, he's so clumsy." Chickie was a squealer, and her high-pitched giggle pierced Arlo's right ear. "He blunders around in here, keeps bumping into me."

Arlo could think of a good reason for bumping into Chickie, but he said nothing. Chickie could take care of herself.

They left together to have a beer in the Square. Old man Guthrie was no longer crouched beside the door waiting to snatch at Arlo as he went by. But as they crossed the overpass they ran into him. He was one of a group of people moving around in the dark, legs and arms appearing in the light of a gasoline lantern, disappearing again. They were working on something, putting up a tent beside a ramshackle structure made of boards.

"Hey, guy, listen, I told you. Hey, guy, come here."

Arlo did not come. "Good night, Guthrie," he said, set-ting off with Chickie in the direction of the Wursthaus on the other side of the Yard. Let Guthrie find another Saint George to fight his battles.

CHAPTER 7

Mary had a baby, oh, Lord,
Mary had a baby, oh, Lord!
Mary had a baby,
Mary had a baby,
Mary had a baby, oh, Lord!
Black American tradition

The production of the Christmas Revels was an enormous undertaking requiring a permanent office in Kendall Square, the year-round attention of a salaried staff, and continuous efforts to raise money. Hundreds of talented people were involved, year after year, paid and unpaid—writers and artists, a music director and a couple of stage directors, a sound engineer, a properties manager, a technical director, a stage manager, a lighting designer, a set designer, a volunteer coordinator, and an organizer of the annual flock of children.

Principal among the talented people was Walter Shattuck, the Old Master, who had begun the Revels years ago, whose singing voice still lent them its haunting mystery. Walt's celebrity was one of the reasons why throngs of people crowded into Memorial Hall to fill Sanders Theatre sixteen times over during every Christmas season. It explained why hordes of volunteers came forward every year to help backstage, to work on costumes and sets, and arrange for tryouts and rehearsal halls, and raise money, and send out mailings.

The volunteers would have explained their loyalty by saying, "Well, I don't know. It's magic. It just, you know, like it casts a spell." Perhaps they were underscoring the researches of Dr. Box, who saw the Revels as a continuation of ancient midwinter rituals and incantations to drive away the fearful darkness. Perhaps, like the mummers and dancers of old, they were whistling to keep up their spirits.

But part of the attraction was surely the magnetism of Sarah Bailey. In the solar system of the Christmas Revels, Sarah was the central sun, sending out her benevolent warmth in all directions. The others circled around her like planets around a star. Her husband, Morgan, was a satellite too, but in a different way. While the others rotated on their own axes, turning away from Sarah and then toward her again and away once more, following their own routines, Morgan was like Mercury—a small and arid planet with one face perpetually facing the sun, his dark side turned to the rest of them, to whatever was not-Sarah.

Morgan's story was complicated, but Sarah's was simple. She had spent a happy childhood climbing into laps, she had grown up easygoing and in love with stories. She had moved comfortably from high school to college to marriage with Morgan, to writing scripts for the Christmas Revels, to becoming one of its stage directors.

Sarah was an optimist. If something wasn't right, she would make it better. If her marriage was troubled, she would fix it. She would cherish Morgan until he trusted her, until he was no longer threatened by the world in which she moved so easily like a fish poising in clear water.

The Revels were wonderful to Sarah. She had no cynicism about them, no doubts. She loved the old songs and tales, she loved the stamping feet of the Morris dancers and the dark spaces of Memorial Hall. In Sanders Theatre the troubles of the world seemed remote and far away. If Sarah had been put in charge of the earth she might have improved it, but that was not her task. This was her job, and she carried it out with grace and confidence in those who worked with her. She mastered the rehearsals without pride or tyranny. With Sarah Bailey in charge, everything seemed simple and straightforward.

But even with Sarah, all was not transparent and truthful. Sarah had an overwhelming secret. She was nearly five months pregnant, but she had told no one. She hadn't even told her husband, Morgan. So far it hadn't been necessary, because she had a lucky shape. Without being fat, she was a thick column of a woman, like those monumental stone goddesses holding up a temple on the Acropolis. Her superb breasts shelved out above her waist. She was large, but she did not look pregnant.

Why hadn't she told Morgan? She would have to tell him soon, because surely she would begin to bulge before long. After all, her husband knew her not only with her clothes on, he knew her naked. How long could she keep her secret? A few weeks? A month?

The trouble was, they had agreed not to have children right away. Morgan needed time, he said, time without distraction. He had work to do. He was making a name for himself as an ornithologist, a comparative anatomist who had written a popular book on bird migration. For a few more years he wanted to be on his own, without depending on teaching, without working for some environmental outfit. He needed to pursue his own researches, wherever they led him. He wanted to write a serious scholarly work.

They would be poor, he said, but they could manage. With children it would be different. He just couldn't handle the confusion and expense of fatherhood right now.

So it wasn't fair to him that this had happened, that she hadn't told him while there was still time to put an end to things. Now it was too late. She wouldn't blame him for being angry.

And something else troubled Sarah. The baby had yet to assert itself by moving inside her. Why didn't it begin to kick and tumble and lash out with its hands and feet? Perhaps it was dead!

"No, no," said the doctor. "Listen, you hear that? It's got a strong heartbeat." Sarah was not reassured. She tried to cheer herself with an image of the baby calmly reading a newspaper under a lighted lamp, just biding its time, but it didn't work. A chill of fear went through her whenever she thought about her child. She kept her fears to herself because she had no one to talk to, but she was constantly aware of the infant in her belly, she was forever asking it to make itself known.

What *would* Morgan say? How would they bear the expense? How could she jeopardize her husband's career so selfishly when he was off to such a good start, when he was already so famous in his own field? How could she?

Her failure to tell her husband was typical of the lack of candor between them. The biggest things never got said.

Sarah had met Morgan Bailey at one of his public lectures. She had come up afterward to ask a question, and he had taken her out to dinner. He was attractive, witty, amusing, and he had the aura that goes with fame. Somehow famous people were more interesting than other people. Sarah had been drawn to him without being able to help herself.

They were married, and for the first year they had been happy together. It didn't matter that Sarah began to be so busy working for the Revels, because Morgan was away most of the time, tracking Canada geese to their breeding grounds in Hudson Bay, then following them south. But this year things were different. Morgan had become so watchful. Whenever Sarah went out, he

wanted to know where. Who would be with her? When would she be back?

Was this the day she should tell him about the baby? No, no, not this morning. Once again Sarah couldn't face it.

She dodged around the kitchen–living room of their apartment on the second floor of the three-decker on Maple Avenue, pulling on her coat and hat, gathering up papers and music and scripts and handbag, pulling on her gloves.

Morgan was already at his desk, but he looked at her sidelong. Oh, God, she was so beautiful. If only she weren't so lovely he wouldn't have to worry. Oh, Christ, he should have married a homely girl, somebody nobody else would look at twice. It was a stab in his side, the way they all stared at her, the way they couldn't take their eyes off her.

It had started slow, this kind of pain in his marriage with Sarah. He told himself it was natural to be a little jealous, perfectly natural. Of course, some jerk of a psychiatrist would call it an obsession. He'd explore Morgan's childhood and uncover the usual traumas of a middle child, he would learn about the radiant intelligence of the older brother who had drowned, and the adorable charm of the younger sister who still lived. But he would never probe deep enough to learn how the drowning had happened, he would never see the agonized drowning face of that good kind brother, so beloved by everyone and afterward so deeply mourned.

The memory of Morgan's older brother was so pinched and puckered with scar tissue and so cauterized with a hot iron that Morgan seldom picked off the scab.

The accident the other day was entirely unrelated, it had nothing to do with it, nothing at all. Morgan admitted to himself that Sarah's preoccupation with the attractive kid from West Virginia had become an anxiety, and then a threat, and finally a torment. But Morgan would never have planned to run over him! The accident had simply happened. There the kid had been, dodging out of Morgan's way, and at once a high excitement had risen in Morgan's head, in his chest, in his arms, in his hands on the steering wheel. It had been so easy, just a twist of the wheel and the kid had gone down!

But the impact had burst open the cauterized scar—the shock of the collision and the ghastly thump of the body beneath the wheels. At once the face of Morgan's drowning brother had reared up in the windshield and the tears of that awful day had burst out in a torrent.

It was all the more strange that he had felt so much bet-

ter the next morning, so calm and serene, so intensely relieved—so glad.

Unfortunately, the serenity was already beginning to
give way—because Sarah didn't have any sense! It was all
her fault, he had seen it at the rehearsal, it was the way
she threw herself at everybody, the way she hugged and
kissed them all. Especially—God!—her codirector, that guy
Tom Cobb. Sarah and Tom were always together, they
were buddies, they were pals, they sat side by side, they
were always touching. *My God, Sarah! Goddamnit, Sarah!*

Morgan looked back at his book without seeing it, and
wrapped his distrust around him like a blanket of thorns.
It lacerated him, it tore at him, but he clutched it tighter.

When Sarah came up behind him and put her arms
around him, he stiffened. She didn't love him, she couldn't
love him. She loved someone else, she loved—

"Oh, Morgan, darling, what are you going to do today?"

At once his suspicions were aroused. Was she trying to discover when he would be out? "Why do you want to know?"

Sarah laughed, and kissed his ear. "I like to think of you,
and know what you're working on when I'm doing something entirely different."

"Oh, well, I guess I'll be in the field part of the time."

"This morning?"

"Yes. No! I mean, I'm not sure." Craftily Morgan hedged
his bets. "I might do it this afternoon." *Don't give her a window of time safe from interruption.*

Sarah had fallen in love with Morgan Bailey because of
his passionate commitment to his field of study, his fasci-
nation with migrating wildfowl—Canada geese and snow
geese and tundra swans. And she loved him for his habit
of mind, which was clever and subtle.

But Sarah was clever too. She saw his trouble as clearly as if he had spoken it aloud. He couldn't hide it. In this matter which had begun to overwhelm him there was nothing witty, nothing subtle. It was a primitive force, huge and dark, blocking out the light.

"What about you?" he said, glancing sideways at her.

"It's an all-day rehearsal. Tom and I have a lot to do. Oh, and that reminds me." Sarah fumbled in her pocketbook. "He asked me to stop at Niki's Market and get him some of those chocolate bars he's so fond of. Oh, God, I've forgotten what they're called. Tastysweets, or something? I wrote it down. Where is it? Oh, here it is. Oh, that's right, Tastychox. Poor Tom, he's got this terrible sweet tooth."

Once again it was Tom Cobb.

"So long, darling. I'll be back about four-thirty." Sarah's feet thumped down the stairs.

It was almost a relief to be alone. Morgan stood up and went to the window and craned his neck. There she was, hurrying to Inman Square to catch the Number 69 bus. When she turned the corner, he sighed, and hunched his shoulders to loosen the tension in his back. Then he pulled the curtains to darken the room, turned on the lamp, and looked over a stack of his own homemade videocassettes. He had recorded the mating of common eiders in Nova Scotia, the nesting of mute swans on the Elizabeth Islands, the rearing of families of great blue herons in the Everglades.

All these things had been worked on by other people, but Morgan's specialty was his gift for noticing simple things, basic things that no one else seemed to see.

Choosing carefully, he plugged in one of his tapes on Canada geese. Canadas were one of the most heavily studied migrating birds in the world, and yet no one had written as thoroughly as Morgan Bailey on the aggressive behavior of the male during the nesting season.

This morning he had a particular reason for looking at this tape. Morgan sat back in the darkened room and watched the pair of geese he had stalked so carefully last May at that little lake in New Hampshire.

There was the female, sitting patiently on her eggs, apparently asleep. Nearby stood the male, his head erect on his long dark neck. Now he stalked along the shore, darting glances left and right, stopping to lower his head and probe for parasites in his tail feathers.

Pretty soon—yes, the zoom lens was picking up the interloper, far away, on the other side of the pond. It was a single male, all by himself, paddling grandly forward. How close would he be allowed to come?

Here was the moment. Morgan's male jerked his neck upright and uttered a honk. Then he took to the water with a rush and lunged at the enemy, eager for battle, beak hissing, wings flapping.

Morgan always laughed at this point, because the other goose backed away as if he were saying, "Excuse *me,* no offense," and took to the air, with Morgan's male in hot pursuit.

The female had been protected. The male had exercised his rights. It was the way any lover would feel when his possession of the female was endangered. He would see it as a threat, he would fend it off, he would keep his mate to himself.

Let the psychiatrists invent their theories. Let them pile theory on theory. The protection of mating rights was instinctive. It was the way of the world. It was natural, perfectly natural.

CHAPTER 8

O master and missus, are you all within?
Pray open the door and let us come in.
O master and missus a-sitting by the fire,
Pray think on us poor travellers,
A-travelling in the mire.

"Somerset Wassail"

The cold had settled in with a vengeance. There had been a few beguiling days at the end of November, days of fraudulent warmth when people thought, *Oh, well, this winter may not be so bad.* Now illusions were shattered. Winter was a hard, bad time. They had forgotten how awful it was. Heavy coats were pulled out of closets. *Oh, God, the moths!* Gloves were exhumed from drawers, the left one missing. *Forty dollars? Just for gloves?* The children had mislaid their winter hats and scarves and mittens, they had forgotten them at school, they had lost them in the rough and tumble of last March. Thermostats were turned up, furnaces roared into life, radiators rattled and steamed, hot air billowed through registers. Oil trucks rumbled up and down the streets of Cambridge.

In Memorial Hall the huge hollow spaces to be heated were as vast as in any cathedral. The dilapidated auditorium where Mary and Homer Kelly taught their classes was often cold. It tended to be forgotten when the building manager twiddled his thermostats in the morning.

The Saturday class was early. At home in Concord they had to get up at six in order to have breakfast and get one of their cold cars going by seven. Then it was a matter of rushing the car up the steep hill beside the Sudbury River, failing to make it the first time, rushing it up again,

hurtling through the woods, tearing down Route 2 to the Alewife parking garage, and boarding the train to Harvard Square.

One of the subway exits in the Square was right beside the Johnson gate, the most pompous of all the entrances to Harvard Yard. This morning the weather in the Yard was even colder than that of the Square. The buildings looked cold too, huge rectangular chunks of brick and stone. People were going to and fro, professors and students bundled against the chilly air, their breath steaming. Burly teenage kids were taking a shortcut to Rindge High. Some sentimental freshman had put a lighted Christmas tree in a second-floor window of Hollis Hall.

Hurrying forward in the direction of Memorial Hall with her arm tucked into Homer's, Mary boldly brought up again her doubts about the accident that had killed Henry Shady. "Listen, Homer, don't you think we should say something to somebody in the Cambridge Police Department about what I heard?"

"What you heard? Oh, you mean the way the brakes squealed at the wrong time?"

"And the way the car was way off the street. And, you know, the goose."

"The goose!" Homer looked at his wife and burst out laughing. "You mean you want to go to an experienced officer of the law who has studied thousands of auto-vehicle accidents in the city of Cambridge and tell him a goose flew over this one? Mary, dear—"

"It's not silly. I heard it. It wasn't just some goose flying from Fresh Pond to the Charles, nothing like that. It was really weird. You know, different."

Homer snickered. "Well, okay, tell him that too. There was this weird goose, this really huge goose, and it flapped up in Henry Shady's face and knocked him down, so the car rolled right over him. And then the goose flew up over Mem Hall and came down on the clock tower and laid an egg."

Mary jerked her arm out of Homer's.

"Well, damnit, I'm sorry. Can't you take a joke? What's happened to you, anyway? You're so prickly lately."

It didn't help. Mary stalked along in stony silence. Not until they had passed through the iron gate onto the overpass above Cambridge Street did she forget her anger. "Homer, look. Something's going on."

There was a village of tents on the overpass. Some were new dome tents in giddy colors, snapped up on plastic stiffening rods, some were old-fashioned tents spiked into the grass with a sledgehammer, one was a huge army tent like a survivor of the First World War. In the middle stood a couple of shacks made of ill-assorted pieces of lumber like flimsy structures knocked together by children in the branches of trees. People were milling around, ducking in and out of the tents. Someone had a noisy ghetto blaster, someone else was trying to squeeze a rolled-up mattress into a pup tent. Beyond Memorial Hall a siren began whining as a fire truck pulled out of the fire station. Was it coming this way? No, the siren was fading. The truck was heading for East Cambridge.

Homer stopped and gawked at the biggest tent. It had a painted sign—

HARVARD TOWERS
COMMAND HEADQUARTERS

"My God," said Homer, "what's this all about?"

"I'll bet I know," said Mary. "Yesterday in Harvard Square—"

HVMANITAS · VIRTVS · PIETAS

AEDIFICATA · ANN · DOM · MDCCCLXXI · ANN · COLL · HARV · CCXXXV

HARVARD TOWERS
COMMAND HEADQUARTERS

But there he was in person, Palmer Nifto, bustling out of the command tent with a sheaf of papers in his hand.

Homer recognized him at once. "Well, Palmer Nifto, hello there. We meet again. Homer Kelly here. Remember a couple of years ago in Concord, when I sprang you and your friends out of jail?"

Palmer grinned at Homer, his breath steaming in the frosty air, and handed him a couple of handbills. "Listen, friend, how'd you like to pin these up someplace? You know, any old place." Homer stared at the handbills, which said,

HARVARD TOWERS
TENT CITY PROTEST
FOR THE HOMELESS CITIZENS OF CAMBRIDGE!
PRESSURE CITY'S BIGGEST LANDLORD,
HARVARD UNIVERSITY!
HARVARD ENDOWMENT:
SIX BILLION DOLLARS!
WE DEMAND
HARVARD REAL ESTATE!

A thickset guy in a Bruins cap approached Palmer Nifto with the end of an extension cord in his hand, yanking it out of a snarled heap of yellow cable. "Where the hell we going to plug in this one?"

Palmer took the plug and looked at Homer and Mary. "Hey, how about you guys plugging this in someplace in Mem Hall? Like we've got all kinds of requirements for electric power. I've got press releases to get out, gotta get my computer going."

Mary was dumbfounded. "Good grief, Palmer, you haven't got a computer in that tent?"

Palmer handed the end of the extension cord to Homer. "Just plug it in anywhere. We've got a couple other outlets, and we're negotiating with the Science Center."

"God, I don't know, Palmer," said Homer, staring doubtfully at the rubber plug in his hand.

"Well, for Christ's sake," said Palmer indignantly. "The students are way ahead of you. They're supplying a power source. I must say it's a sad day when the older generation is too timid for the courageous actions of the young." Nifto pointed to a plump young man approaching from Phillips Brooks House, carrying a tray of doughnuts. "Welcome, Scottie," he shouted. "What have you got there?"

The plump young man was at once surrounded by eager takers. Mary recognized some of them. She had seen the hugely pregnant young teenager in Porter Square. The old man who never stopped talking usually sat on the sidewalk in front of the Harvard Coop. And here was the other old man, the one who never spoke, who huddled beside the subway entrance at Church Street and turned up sometimes on the steps to their own classroom. Some of the others were familiar too, people who sold newspapers on the street, and the guy on Rollerblades who swooped like a dancer in and out among the cars on Massachusetts Avenue. They were homeless, all these people. Until now they must have been spending the night in local shelters.

"But, Palmer," said Mary, "it's wintertime. You people aren't sleeping here, are you? Not overnight?"

"The Peasants' Revolt," proclaimed a loud voice at Mary's elbow. It was Dr. Box in her purple hat, surveying the scene, casting it into historical perspective. "Wat Tyler defying the king. A chancy business," she said, scowling at Palmer Nifto. "Do you know what happened to Wat Tyler?"

Palmer Nifto reached out to grab the last two doughnuts from Scottie's tray, but Mary adroitly snatched one of them, while Dr. Box cried, "Murder! That's what happened to Wat Tyler!"

"Won't you take it?" said Mary, holding out the doughnut to the old man in the blanket.

For a moment she thought the old black man was asleep, but then his hand crept out and took the morsel from her fingers, and snaked back out of sight.

"Well, okay, Palmer," said Homer, "I'll see what I can do." With Mary's help he dragged a length of sixteen connected extension cords across the brick and asphalt and grass of the overpass into the lecture hall, and found an outlet at the back. Guiltily, taking leave of his senses, he plugged it into the wall.

Mary put down her briefcase and hugged her coat around her. "He forgot again. It's cold as ice in here."

Homer had taught his last class in overcoat and mittens, while the students huddled in their seats, their fingers too cold to take notes. They had scuttled out before his favorite joke. "Damnit, I talked to the manager. He promised it wouldn't happen again."

"If we lived in the Congo with the Musurongo," said Mary, thinking of Dr. Box, "we'd be basking in jungle heat right now."

Homer shuffled his papers, trying to find his part of the morning lecture. He couldn't concentrate. He was remembering what Mary had said yesterday: *I sometimes wonder how our ancestors survived the winter. How did they keep themselves alive?*

"Are you ready, Homer? It's your turn first."

Homer wasn't ready, and kids were beginning to come in and take off their jackets and settle down and open their notebooks. In his head he saw a bonfire, somewhere in the cold northland, some time in prehistory. People were dancing around the fire in the polar dusk, with the sun barely skimming the horizon and beginning to sink. They were howling, tonking on kettles, ringing wild bells, and the combined racket, the crashing rattle of the pots, the crazed vibration of the hollow bells, mounted to the sky to summon back the sun. And the sun heard it, and condescended to obey. Slowly and reluctantly at first, but then with increasing power and strength, it shone longer every day, until at last it warmed and loosened the frozen ground.

"Come on, Homer," whispered Mary, "shape up. Everybody's waiting."

On that December morning, thirteen days before the shortest day of the year, there were fifteen tents and one shack on the grassy islands of the overpass. And more shelters were popping up, antic constructions with flimsy supports and drooping canvas walls. The tent city was catching on.

CHAPTER 9

We bring you love, the faithful light
Of dawn that comes to end the night;
Sing we Noël, Noël, Noël!
                    Carol, "Sing We Noël"

A rlo's work was like a thicket into which he could burrow, a private place of his own. Unlocking the door of Room 804 in the Science Center was like entering the hollow place in the middle of the thicket. This morning he was glad to find himself alone. His colleague Harley Finch was elsewhere. Of course Harley was clever enough at his own line of expertise, but in Arlo's opinion he was an ambitious bastard, and too nosy into the bargain. He always seemed less interested in his own stuff than in whatever Arlo was up to.

The day was bright and sunny. Arlo inspected his silent camera. It was an ordinary-looking big box camera with a plateholder, a ninety-millimeter wide-angle lens, a digital alarm clock, and an electronic shutter attachment. This morning everything looked the same as usual.

In four days, if all went well, the shutter would open at eight-thirty in the morning for the next-to-last exposure of the sun. Then, on the twenty-second of December, it would click open once again to record the lowest point in the sun's annual journey.

But that wasn't all. There would still be another exposure, different from the rest. After the last shot of the sun on the twenty-second, Arlo would remove the filter and set the clock to take a picture of Memorial Hall on the same afternoon. The result would be an extraordinary

multiple-image picture of the tower of Mem Hall in the afternoon sunlight, and behind it the great figure eight of the
sun's changing position in the sky throughout an entire
year, forty-four bright suns in a double loop.

From beginning to end the lens must be aimed in precisely the same direction. Arlo squinted through the rifle-
sight scope. It still showed him the northeastern finial on
the top of the tower, and the feet of the tripod were still
firmly taped to the floor. It was important that they stay
that way. If anything happened to joggle them, the last solar images would be out of line.

Then he turned to the spectrohelioscope. The heliostat
on the terrace was a clock-driven sun-tracking mirror that
sent back an image through the big window to another
mirror, on the rear wall, which flashed it to a third mirror,
which sent it to the spectrohelioscope, which sorted out
its light and dropped a solar image on the observing table
below.

This morning the image was full of detail, boiling
slowly like a bowl of oatmeal in the light of the alpha line
of hydrogen. Like the minute hand of a clock, the move-
ment of the granules was almost fast enough to be per-
ceived by the eye, but not quite.

Here on this sheet of paper was the object of all Arlo's
studies—oh, not this big blank photosphere with the
blotch of sunspots on its face, but the deeper levels below
the surface, with their mysteriously reversing pulsations.
Arlo had studied solar oscillations at the Big Bear solar observatory in California, and last winter he had joined an
expedition to the Antarctic to observe the sun in uninter-
rupted daylight.

The analemma project and the spectrohelioscope were
simple matters, unrelated to Arlo's pulsation researches.

They were teaching tools for his students. The real attraction that drew him to the eighth floor of the Science Center every day was the computer with which he was analyzing data from his own Antarctic observations of periodic solar oscillations.

Of course, it was mostly number-crunching, but Arlo didn't care. Ninety-nine percent of one's working life was mechanical routine. It was the remaining 1 percent that made it all worthwhile, the precious 1 percent that formed the drifting visions of his mind in sleep, the undercurrent of his thoughts as he pushed his tray along the line in the cafeteria downstairs or sat around in Sanders Theatre waiting for his turn to take the part of Saint George.

Arlo zipped up his parka and left the lab, leaving the door unlocked for Chickie Pickett. He had an appointment with the chairman of the astronomy department, over there on Garden Street, in one of the old observatory buildings.

He left the Science Center by the west door. Looking back at the mall over Cambridge Street, he was surprised to see a cluster of tents. Last night there had been only one or two.

What was going on? It must be some kind of homeless protest. For a moment Arlo stopped to watch. He was amused to see a figure he recognized as Guthrie grabbing at a passerby. No, it wasn't just a passerby, it was an officer of the Harvard Police Department. What the hell would they do about Guthrie and his homeless friends and all those shacks and tents?

Then Arlo forgot Guthrie in the tricky business of crossing Massachusetts Avenue to Cambridge Common and negotiating Garden Street. On the corner where First Congregational Church reared its stone steeple, a few home-

less men were leaving the church shelter. A procession of
church women streamed past Arlo, carrying trays of hot
food in the direction of Palmer Nifto's tent city. In their
flapping coats they were an argosy in full sail.

Arlo nodded at the women, but he was thinking about
his own problems, not those of the fragile village between
the Science Center and the Yard. There was a rumor of an
approaching cutback in the astronomy department. Who
would be asked to leave? Who but the junior members of
the staff, Harley Finch and Arlo Field?

"One of us or both of us?" Arlo had said to Harley. "Do
you think they'll knock off you and me?"

Harley had not wanted to discuss it. "Jesus," he mumbled, "I hope to God they don't go through with it."

Arlo didn't waste time thinking about it. He was content to bide his time with his own future, his own life. He
would find his level sooner or later. But he couldn't help
noticing Harley's new habit of hanging around the office
of the chairman of the department. Was he currying favor,
or what?

The observatory complex was a collection of buildings
on a hilltop between Concord Avenue and Garden Street.
Once upon a time it had made use of its famous telescope,
the Great Refractor, but in the polluted atmosphere of
Cambridge the old instrument had long since become a
historical curiosity. Astronomy on Observatory Hill was
no longer optical. It was X-ray, gamma ray, radio astronomy, using instruments scattered all over the world and
on satellites high above the earth.

But some of the observatory's old functions were still
going strong. Arlo dropped in to say hello to Johnny
Mitchell in the tiny office of the Central Bureau for Astronomical Telegrams. Johnny was in charge of a clearing-

house for information about comets and novae and black holes and variable stars. As Arlo looked in his door, Johnny's telephone was ringing, his computer screen was reporting the arrival of electronic mail, and paper was coming out of his fax machine.

Johnny nodded at Arlo and picked up the phone. "Right," he said, "gotcha. R. Coronae Borealis, magnitude estimate 6.7. This was last night, right? Right."

Arlo grinned at Johnny and headed for the chairman's office, passing chambers sacred to Harvard astronomical history—the Library of Glass Plates, the room that had been Harlow Shapley's. In the chairman's office he found an ominous sign of trouble. Harley Finch was there before him, in close conversation with the chairman.

Startled, they backed away from each other and stared at him. Harley moved his arm behind his back as if he were hiding something. They were like a couple of kids caught smoking behind the barn.

"Well, hello there, Arlo," said the chairman heartily. "What can I do for you?"

"Oh, sorry, I thought we had an appointment."

"Whoops," said the chairman, flipping open his calendar.

"It doesn't matter," said Arlo. "I'll come back another time." Turning to leave, he caught a glimpse of the object behind Harley's back. It looked familiar. Its shiny cover was like the one attached to his report on his work at Kitt Peak last summer.

Why were they whispering about his summer report? It had been blameless enough. Well, maybe its blamelessness could itself be blamed. Arlo had been too unimportant to be permitted a lot of time with the McMath solar telescope, and therefore he hadn't accomplished much science of his own.

He left the office wondering if he should look for other employment. If they were about to fire somebody, it would surely be Arlo Field. Harley Finch would make sure of that.

◇ ◇ ◇ ◇ ◇ ◇ ◇ ◇ ◇ ◇ ◇ ◇

PART TWO

THE BOAST

No one could ever frighten me,
For many I have slain.
I long to fight,
'Tis my delight
To battle once again.
      Saint George and the Dragon

◇ ◇ ◇ ◇ ◇ ◇ ◇ ◇ ◇ ◇ ◇ ◇

CHAPTER 10

I'll pierce thy body full of holes and make thy buttons fly.
Traditional British Mummers' Play

The officer inspecting Palmer Nifto's tent city was not employed by the city of Cambridge. Sumner Plover was a member of the Harvard Police Department. He was one of sixty-three sworn officers who had attended the Massachusetts Training Council Academy for firearms training and instruction in the general laws of Massachusetts.

Sumner was a trusted and experienced officer, but this time he was very late in discovering what was going on.

The overpass was part of his North Yard territory, but it was invisible from his cruiser. His territory was too big, that was the trouble. Officer Plover was responsible for patrolling the Law School and the Littauer School of Government on Massachusetts Avenue and the residence halls on Everett Street and a long stretch of Oxford Street with all its science buildings—McKay Laboratory and Mallinckrodt, the Museum of Comparative Zoology and the great glass edifice of the Science Center—and on Divinity Avenue the biological laboratories and the University Herbarium and William James Hall, and farther to the east the Yenching Library and the Semitic Museum and Hillel House and the Divinity School. It was an awful lot to keep track of.

Sumner didn't know much about the insides of all these buildings except for the glass flowers in the Museum of Comparative Zoology—everybody knew about the glass flowers. Sumner had a college degree from Boston Univer-

sity, but he had avoided math and science as much as possible, and as for the theological part of his beat, his own
religion was a long way from that of the wild radicals in
the Divinity School.

But he felt an instinctive respect for the diversity of
teaching and research going on around him. One of his
friends in the other police department, the one belonging
to the city of Cambridge, was always referring to Harvard
professors as double-domed assholes, but not Sumner
Plover. After all, some of these scientists had won Nobel
Prizes. It pleased him to think that his own part of the university was pushing back the frontiers of scientific knowledge. On his day off he sometimes drove his wife around
his district, telling her the names of the buildings and their
special requirements for security. Bonnie loved the glass
flowers.

But his intimacy with the neighborhoods of the North
Yard had failed him this time. The mall over Cambridge
Street was largely invisible from the corner of Kirkland
and Oxford Streets, where his cruiser patrolled every day.
And therefore Sumner did not learn about the tent city until it had been in existence for two whole days, when his
intercom suddenly burst into scratchy life while he was
moseying around the MCZ parking lot, looking for cars
without the right kind of sticker.

It was the sergeant who was his patrol supervisor.
"Woman named Box reports tents on the overpass. She
sounds like a nutcase, but maybe you'd better look into it.
Name of the party in charge is Tyler, Wat Tyler."

So it was not until then, far too late for prompt removal,
that Sumner discovered to his horror the wooden shack
and the nine tents, and the throngs of homeless people and
students and hangers-on, and the tangled lengths of exten-

sion cord and the open mike and the interference with the pedestrian crosswalk of the new encampment called Harvard Towers.

As he stood gaping, a truck pulled up, its flatbed filled with tall blue Portapotties. There were cheers and whistles. The truck driver grinned and yelled, "Where do you want 'em?"

"Hold it, hold it," shouted Sumner, waving his arms. "Is there somebody here named Tyler?"

Nobody was listening. They were all gathering around the Portapotty truck, which was backing up carefully beside the hedge, while a tall guy in dark glasses walked backward beside it, beckoning with both hands. He was obviously in charge.

Sumner adopted his most authoritative manner. "Is your name Tyler? Listen here—" And then he saw his mistake. "No, no, you're not Tyler. I've seen you before. You're Palmer Nifto, right? Well, I'm afraid I must ask you and your friends to leave."

Palmer smiled, and stepped back to watch the descent of the Portapotties onto the frozen grass. Turning his in-

scrutable dark shades on Sumner, he said mildly, "May I
ask what you think you're doing? Harvard Police, right?
Well, listen, friend, it's my understanding this overpass is
the property of the city of Cambridge. Therefore, you have
no right to evict us. I should warn you we are represented
by legal counsel." Palmer raised his voice. "Hey, Frank,
you got your camera?"

Frank was a heavyset young guy with a bald head and
yellow whiskers. He came running, snapping pictures of
Officer Plover and Palmer Nifto as he ran.

Sumner stared at the camera openmouthed. Then he
collected himself. "Your electric power—may I ask where
it comes from? It doesn't matter who owns this property if
you're stealing power from Harvard University."

Palmer folded his arms. "Get Gretchen over here, will
you?" he said to Frank.

"Hey, Gretchen," bawled Frank.

Gretchen appeared at once, struggling out of a small tent.
She was a very young girl in the last stages of pregnancy.

Sumner was trapped. He didn't back away in time. It
took Frank only a minute to push Gretchen between him
and Palmer Nifto and record for posterity the confronta-
tion of police power with a homeless young mother-to-be.

"Good," said Nifto. "Now, can you get it to the *Cambridge Chronicle* right away?"

Afterward, when Sumner made his report about the in-
cident to the sergeant at headquarters on Garden Street,
he was almost speechless. "Like he raised the question, did
the overpass belong to Harvard or the city of Cambridge? I
didn't know who the hell it belonged to."

"We're too late, that's the trouble," said the patrol supervisor gloomily. "We should have got in there as soon as
they put up the first tent."

"But suppose he's right? Suppose the overpass does belong to the city? I mean, the tunnel underneath where the traffic goes through, that must be Cambridge, right?"

"Oh, God," said the supervisor. "I'll find out. I'll call the office of Harvard's General Counsel." He shook his head sadly at Sumner. "We should have evicted them first thing, not given them a chance to take hold."

"I know." Guiltily Sumner remembered the breezy way he had swept his cruiser around the curve of Oxford Street. He should have parked the car, he should have walked around the building to the overpass, he should have found this little canker at the very beginning, before it metastasized into a tumor on the body of the university, before it became a Problem with a capital P. He should have said, *Out! Get out of here right now, you hear me? Get this tent out of here before I call the Chief of Harvard Police.*

But he hadn't, and it was too late now.

"Who else should we notify?" said Sumner's supervisor, with his hand on the phone. "The Harvard Planning Of-

fice‹ Wait, I know. I'll call Community Affairs. They're the ones should be handling a thing like this. What's that guy's name, the Vice-President in charge of Government and Community Affairs‹ Hernshaw, something like Hernshaw‹"

"Henshaw, I think," said Sumner. "His name is Ernest Henshaw."

CHAPTER 11

Here comes I that never come yit,
With my big head and my little wit.
Traditional British Mummers' Play

Sometimes one can think of marriage as a seesaw. Ideally, the husband and wife should be evenly balanced at the two ends.

But there are marriages in which it is the husband who possesses all the intellectual and psychological weight, so that his end of the plank is solidly, firmly on the ground, while his noodle-headed wife sits mooning aloft.

And there are others in which the situation is reversed. It was so with the marriage of Harvard's Vice-President in charge of Government and Community Affairs. Mr. and Mrs. Ernest Henshaw were no longer a well-matched pair. It was Helen Henshaw's common sense and commanding ways that now ran the household.

Not that Ernest was a failure—nothing of the sort. In his long attachment to Harvard University he had been highly successful in moving up from one administration post to another, until now he was very high indeed, with an office in Massachusetts Hall, in the same building as the office of the President. At the moment the President was away on sabbatical, but Helen Henshaw was proud that his empty rooms were close to the ones occupied by her husband.

She too was successful. Helen was an interior decorator with a budding practice among her friends and neighbors. Her own house on Berkeley Street was a perfect advertisement. It stood in a little enclave behind the Episcopal Divinity School. All her friends wanted living rooms and bedrooms and bathrooms just like Helen's. Her style was bouffant and bedecked with pillows, it was choked with flowery sofas, flouncy draperies, hanging plants, enormous lamps, canopied beds, patchwork quilts, antique dolls, duck decoys, old clocks, copper pots, ornamental chess sets, statuettes, and china dogs.

On the day the Portapotty truck arrived at Harvard Towers, a van pulled into the Henshaw driveway to deliver two pieces of antique furniture. When Ernest saw them in the dining room, he complained to his wife, "There isn't room in here for those cupboards. They're blocking the door to the hall."

"They're not cupboards, they're armoires."

"They're what?"

"Armoires, it's French, and the other door provides a perfectly adequate flow of traffic."

Ernest said nothing more. Helen had won. She always got her way about the decoration of the house, because after all it was her business. Helen was happy in her new profession, but in her domestic life she was becoming more and more uneasy. It was beginning to be transparently clear that Ernest was no longer the man she had married.

One day she came upon him in her bedroom groping in a bureau drawer.

"Ernest, what on earth are you doing?"

"Counting," mumbled Henshaw.

"Counting?" His wife stared at his crouched back. "You're counting my underwear?"

"Everything. I'm counting everything in this house. I want to find out how many things we own."

"Oh, I see. Do you think I have too much underwear, Ernest?"

"No, no, it isn't that." Absently Henshaw wrote down the number of his wife's slips and panties and girdles and brassieres and nightgowns. He was thinking of his great-great-great-grandfather, who had lived in rural Maine in the latter part of the eighteenth century. A list of his possessions had come down in the family:

1 blue great coat	3 sickles
1 fine shirt	2 pails and piggin
2 woosted caps	1 pair horse traces and hames
1 feather bed	1 plow share
6 joiners chairs	1 dung fork
1 case of draws	1 horse
1 gridiron	3 cows
1 teakittle	1 heifer calf
2 brine tubs	600 weight of live hogs

Count them, that was twenty-five things his great-great-great-grandfather had owned, plus a horse, three cows, a calf, and two or three hogs. In his own house two centuries later, in an inventory of the kitchen alone he had listed 1,252 separate items.

He poked in a cupboard. "What's this basket here?"

"It happens to be my sewing basket."

Under his wife's eye, Henshaw inspected the basket. There were nineteen spools of thread, three thimbles, a paper of snaps, another of hooks and eyes and one of needles, a packet of bias tape, and a pincushion with a multitude of pins.

"Ernest, what on earth are you doing with my pincushion?"

"Counting the pins."

"Ernest!"

CHAPTER 12

And once more came the lady sweet
To stir Sir Gawain's dreams. . . .
  "Sir Gawain and the Green Knight"

Morgan Bailey sat up in bed. It was too early to get up, but his perpetual wariness had awakened him, as though it were necessary to keep watch against an invader in the bedroom, someone who might creep slyly under the covers and make love to Sarah.

Of course, that was absurd. But his vision of the night had put him on guard. He had been dreaming about the girl who lived downstairs, Chickie Pickett. Chickie was a graduate student doing some kind of astronomical dissertation, living with a roommate. Morgan and Chickie met sometimes on the front porch, coming or going. The roommate was a student of feminist theology at the Divinity School. She was sociable and talkative, but it was Chickie's curvaceous loveliness that attracted Morgan. In his dream he had been tearing off her clothes, carrying her to bed, fondling her, passionately kissing her.

The dream was only a goad to his fears about Sarah. If *he* had dreams like that, surely she did too.

If only she had some sense! If only she knew friend from foe, lamb from tiger. She was so stupid! She was always throwing her arms around people, making them think she was ready for any adventure, like those women in the personal columns, *Good-time girl,* meaning hot and ready to fuck. He had warned her, he had told her over and over, *For Christ's sake, Sarah, hold back, show a little common sense!*

72

He looked down at her now, lying there beside him, her face so fresh and soft, her features blurred by sleep, her thick hair spread all over the pillow. She was smiling.

Why was she smiling? Was she dreaming about someone? Who was it? Tom Cobb? "Sarah," Morgan whispered, "wake up."

Sarah sighed, and murmured something, then turned over on her side, still asleep.

What had she said? Was it someone's name? Morgan shook her arm. "What did you say? Sarah, wake up!"

"Oh, Morgan, dear, what is it?" Sarah lifted her head and looked at him.

Morgan repented. She was so drowsy, so innocent! "Nothing, it's nothing." He lay down and turned away from her.

Sarah snuggled against his back, and fell asleep again.

Oh, Christ, what was she dreaming now?

It galled him, it seared him, that he could not control his wife's dreams.

Tuesday morning, and there was to be a technical rehearsal of the Revels. At the breakfast table Sarah made notes on her script. Morgan looked at her cautiously, and tried to sound offhand. "Do you mind if I come along?"

Sarah looked up in surprise. "I thought you were going to spend the day in the field? I thought you said it was important?"

"Oh, well, it doesn't really matter." But Morgan knew it did matter. He wanted to catch the moment when the Canadas took off for good, when they stopped going from pond to pond and went south in earnest. It wouldn't be long now. In this cold weather most inland lakes were frozen over. Soon the geese would stop their noisy descents to the few remaining spaces of open water, they would no longer graze in the stubbled cornfields. They would take off for the last time, squawking and shouting, heading south.

But Morgan couldn't bear the idea that Sarah would be spending the entire day in the company of Tom Cobb. Tom had grown taller in Morgan's mind, his black hair was curlier, his muscular shoulders were broader, his encroachment on the territory that was Sarah Bailey was ever more dangerous.

"But you explained it to me," said Sarah, "how important it is, trying to catch the day they fly away."

"I know, that's what I said, but I'd really like to see—you know—the way the performance begins to come together."

Sarah looked at her husband and guessed what was troubling him. She smiled and reached across the table to take his hand. "All right, then, come on. We'll walk over together."

For a moment Morgan's bluff was called. Then his new protective intelligence took over. His jealousy had made him smarter. Spikes of cleverness bristled from his head like thorns of glass. "No, no, you're right. You go ahead. I'll drive out to Concord. The geese have been coming down on the cornfield on Route 117. If they leave there, I'll try Fairhaven Bay and Flint's Pond, all the usual places. Maybe this time they'll take off and not come back."

The thing was, if he spent the day with Sarah, he wouldn't see anything. If she knew he was there, she'd be careful. Morgan wanted to see what she was like when she thought he was nowhere near. Could he trust her? No, no! He couldn't trust her!

So he waited only a moment after Sarah clattered down the stairs before hauling on his jacket and following her.

Mary Kelly spotted the two of them as she strolled along Cambridge Street, coming away from Niki's Market, where she had bought a couple of sandwiches. It struck her as odd—Sarah was hurrying on ahead, with Morgan hastening after her half a block behind. Look at him! He was pausing, watching Sarah, not trying to catch up. How very strange. At once Mary's pop psychology reasserted itself. Should she tell Homer? No, he would laugh and she'd get mad again. She was mad already, in anticipation. Better shut up.

But a few minutes later, in Sanders Theatre, Mary saw Morgan's shadowy figure on the upper balcony, nearly hidden behind the woodwork supporting the wooden vault. Watching, he was still watching.

Then Mary forgot Morgan Bailey as the technical director got to work trying different effects of lighting, moving his switches up and down, adding here and subtracting there. He called to Sarah, "Hey, Sarah, where's Tom?"

"Sick today," said Sarah. "I was supposed to meet him for breakfast, but they had a message. He's down with a stomach bug. We'll have to get along without him."

The tech director laughed. "A stomach bug, it's all that chocolate. God, that guy sure has a sweet tooth. Hey, Sarah, how's this for 'The Moon Shines Bright'?"

The lighting effects were for Walter Shattuck, the Old Master. He stood on the stage with spotlights playing over him. "No, not the yellow," said Sarah. "Wait, I like the blue one."

Then Walt began to sing. Mary Kelly, listening from the mezzanine, understood once again that everything in the Revels hung on the thread of Walt's voice—all the singers and dancers, all the mummers, all the Morris men with their sticks and swords. Even the rising tiers of seats in

Sanders Theatre seemed spellbound, and the great bulk of Memorial Hall itself. Whatever was foolish in the Revels, whatever was artificial, vanished as he sang—

> *The moon shines bright and the stars give a light*
> *A little before it is day;*
> *Our Lord our God He called on us*
> *And bids us awake and pray.*

It was a voice that summoned the ghosts of men and women who had sung in village streets in Scotland and England and Wales, in Kentucky and Tennessee—men black from the mines of Northumberland or West Virginia, girls crowned with flowers in the Cotswolds, hunters in Abbots Bromley blessing the deer, lusty men in Ireland singing for pennies at cottage doors. He sang them into being without antiquarian fuss, without the pedagogical moralizing of Dr. Box. He sang simply, and the years rolled back and all times and places were one—

> *Awake! O awake, good people all,*
> *Awake, and you shall hear:*
> *Our Lord, our God was born on this day*
> *For us whom He loved so dear.*

The song came to an end, and Mary glanced up to see if Morgan Bailey was still up there on the second balcony keeping an eye on his wife.

No, he was gone.

CHAPTER 13

The lord rode forth to hunt the fox
Before the next day's beams.
"Sir Gawain and the Green Knight"

Morgan drove out to Concord with relief in his breast. Tom Cobb was not going to be with Sarah, not today, because he was sick. Morgan grinned to himself. Sick from eating candy bars! Poor self-indulgent bastard.

Smiling, Morgan turned off the Concord Turnpike and headed through the town of Lincoln in the direction of Route 117. It was a good day for winter fieldwork. The weather was surprisingly warm. All those homeless people on the mall outside Mem Hall had been standing around outside their tents or sitting on folding chairs in the milky sunshine. But the tent city couldn't last long. A little more bitter weather like last week, or one big snowstorm, and they'd be gone.

The geese too would enjoy the balmy winter day. In weather like this they'd be unlikely to leave for good. Of course, if they did, if they flew south on a day like this, it would mean something important. It would mean that the amount of daylight was more important than the temperature.

The question was complex. Why *did* a flock at last make up its mind to leave? Morgan was keeping track, comparing notes from year to year, trying to associate the migration with the weather, with the food supply, with human interference, with disasters of one kind of another.

As he approached the cornfield, he began to worry.

What if they had flown already? But they were still there, the same big flock, moving slowly around the field, gleaning the detritus left from the harvested stalks.

Morgan had a sheltered parking place in the woods. He left his car and approached carefully, moving among the trees beside the field, looking for the path that led to the river, keeping the birds in view.

But suddenly they took off. With a wild croaking and shouting and a flapping of great dark wings, they lifted from the ground and flew away, making a hoarse clamor over the river.

What had disturbed them? Surely it wasn't his fault? Was it somebody else, blundering too close?

Then Morgan caught a glimpse of the marauder. A fox was running off with a goose in its mouth. It was heading straight for Morgan.

He yelled as it went by, and the shocked fox dropped the goose and ran away, skimming through the cornfield, a floating flash of color, the white band on its tail visible after the rest merged with the undergrowth.

The goose was dead. Morgan bent down and turned it over. Its neck was bloody and broken. Its round black eye looked up at him blindly. And then he cursed. There was a green band on the bird's left leg. It was his own band, the one he had fastened to the male of the nesting pair he had studied last spring. *Shit!*

Morgan looked up, and was not surprised to see another bird circling above him, looking down, uttering plaintive cries. It was the female who had laid her clutch of eggs and tended them until they hatched, then guarded the four goslings all summer, paddling behind them while the male took the lead. The female too was banded. What would happen to her now?

In a rage Morgan left the dead goose on the ground and hurried to his car. In a moment he was back with a little jar of dark paste and a table knife. The paste was something he kept in the trunk, a useful mixture of peanut butter and arsenate of lead.

Bending over the goose, he dipped the knife in the jar and spread the dark stuff all over the injured neck. "Shoo!" he shouted at the hovering goose, which was still circling, landing nearby, and taking off again.

Carefully and thoroughly Morgan pressed the poisoned knife deep into the open wound. When the fox came back to his kill, he would find a little surprise.

Time now to look for the flock somewhere else. Morgan ran back to his car and returned the deadly jar to the padlocked toolbox in the trunk. As he drove away in the direction of White's Pond, he understood why he felt so bereft. The two banded geese had been special birds. They were the very pair whose behavior he had recorded last spring with his video camera. The powerful action of the male was Morgan's justification, his argument, his vindication, his defense. Its behavior under threat was written in the chromosome chains, emblazoned in the stars. It was the way of the world. It was normal.

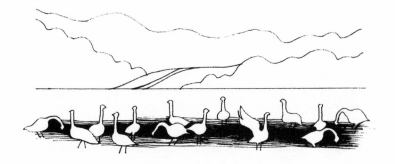

CHAPTER 14

Oh, good man and good wife, are you within?
Pray lift the latch and let us come in.
We see you a-sitting at the boot o' the fire,
Not a-thinkin' of us in the mud and the mire,
So it's joy be to you and a jolly wassail!

Kentucky wassail

The residents of Harvard Towers were a mixed lot. Palmer Nifto had gathered them up from all over, beginning with old friends he had met in shelters here and there.

For reasons of public relations, his favorite was Gretchen Milligan. Gretchen was a slightly retarded nineteen-year-old girl with a plump childish face. She had given birth already to two children, and turned them over at once for adoption. She was about to have another. Gretchen knew that pregnancy was a useful condition for a homeless woman. When you got beyond the second trimester there were benefits, and you could stay at Bright Day House in Somerville, a home for unmarried pregnant teenagers. It was warm and comfortable at Bright Day, and the food was good.

When her time came, she would certainly get herself right over there in a taxi. But for now she would stay at Harvard Towers to support the cause. Gretchen was really impressed by Palmer Nifto's leadership. Harvard was going to give them apartments, that was what Palmer said. He said he had Harvard wrapped around his little finger.

And she liked being right here in the middle of Harvard College. Gretchen had a taste for dignity and grandeur, for the finer things, for fancy doorways with white columns and iron gates with vases on top. She loved to trail along the streets in the elegant part of Cambridge and look at the beautiful houses—oh, not just on Brattle Street! Gretchen had made wonderful discoveries on some of the side streets. Nobody else knew about them, the little secret corners where the luckiest people lived.

Somehow Harvard College and the big houses on Gretchen's secret streets had something in common, a distinction, a kind of majesty. It was something she yearned for.

Of course, the people at Bright Day were after her. They found her right away at Harvard Towers. "Gretchen," her counselor said, "you're almost due. It's not good for your baby for you to be out in the cold like this. What if you couldn't get to us in time? What if you delivered your baby on the street? And, Gretchen, you're missing your group discussions, you're not doing your chores."

But Gretchen was loyal to Palmer Nifto. "We need you, Gretchen," Palmer kept saying. "You're the most impor-tant person at Harvard Towers."

She knew her big belly helped the cause. Already she had been photographed by the *Cambridge Chronicle* and the *Cambridge Tab* and the *Harvard Crimson* and even by the *Harvard Gazette*. She had stuck her stomach out proudly, and now she was going to be on TV, because yesterday a crew from Channel 4 had come to Harvard Towers and Palmer had pushed her right out in front.

Bob Chumley was an old regular from the chancy world of Cambridge homelessness. He was smart and capable and could lend his hand to anything, but an addiction to cocaine kept him from holding down a job. Bob was unac-ceptable in the shelters of Cambridge, because he had a couple of dogs, big handsome golden retrievers, and you couldn't have dogs in a shelter.

Guthrie Jones was a homeless man whose beat was Harvard Square. There was a fey charm about Guthrie, but you had to be on the lookout or he would talk your ear off, wanting to tell you something, something that could never be quite articulated, something terribly important if only he could utter it, some anguished fury against the world.

Linda Bunting should never have been homeless at all, because she was the mother of two small children. Somehow she had dropped through the cracks of the welfare system. She had a nice tent full of stuffed toys and sleeping bags, and a space heater blasting out its orange comfort twenty-four hours a day. And the children were perfectly warm. Their tiny noses barely showed between knitted hats and woolly scarves.

Some of the other citizens of Harvard Towers were less beguiling. Oh, Vergil Taylor was all right. He made good copy, because he almost never took off his Rollerblades. Vergil skimmed around the edges of the tent city and rattled over the uneven surfaces of the brick walks and whizzed along the asphalt paths of Harvard Yard, swooping in graceful arcs, leaning left, leaning right, in a perpetual dance. He made a good courier whenever Palmer had an urgent message to deliver.

The only other Afro-American at Harvard Towers was old Albert Maggody. No one knew his history. No one had ever heard him speak. Maggody took no part in tent-city activities and he made no response to questions. He just sat there, wrapped in layers of blankets, his face nearly hidden. Only his hand appeared when someone passed a tray of sandwiches or proffered a cup of coffee. He never said, *Bless you,* like some of them. Maggody was life at its lowest terms.

To Mary Kelly, who was beginning to take an interest in the occupants of Harvard Towers, his was the most pitiful case.

One of the homeless women was a problem for Palmer Nifto. Of course he welcomed one and all, because he was anxious to increase the population of Harvard Towers, but Emily Pollock gave him a pain. Emily had been a flower child in the seventies, but now she was a fat bossy woman in giant earrings and full skirts and big woolly caftans. She was always offering screwy advice, and making decisions without consulting Palmer first, then screeching them to the world on the open mike. "We're going to organize a council," bawled Emily, "and run this place democratically from now on."

Palmer had no intention of handing over his authority to a democratic council. And when a delegation from United Harvard Ministries came to him, representing the pastors of a number of local churches, he was distinctly cool.

"Our coffeehouse is open to all comers," said the minister of First Parish Unitarian, smiling at him graciously.

"Our public-relations expertise is at your service," suggested the clergyman from First Church Congregational, his face bright with sympathy.

"Our copy machine is yours to command," said the rector from Christ Church. "And our bathrooms are always open." He made a joke. "We call it our Latrine Ministry."

"You must know about our free dinners," said the priest from Saint Paul's. "Some of our churches serve dinner to all comers one night a week. Monday at Massachusetts Avenue Baptist in Inman Square, Tuesday at First Parish Unitarian in Harvard Square, Wednesday—"

Palmer would have none of it. "Thanks," he said, "but no thanks."

The truth was, he didn't want to share his ragtag glory with any of these clever and powerful people. Oh, the churchwomen were all right, the ones who brought food— big containers of soup and coffee and spaghetti, laundry baskets of sandwiches, big bags of muffins and cookies. And the girl who collected leftovers from local restaurants was okay too—the day-old croissants from Au Bon Pain, the sausages and cheeses from the Wursthaus, and the vichyssoise from the Stockpot. Actually, there was a run on vichyssoise, and people were complaining. "Oh, no, not vichyssoise again."

Palmer himself was a clever escapee from alimony and child support. He had been living by his wits on the street for years. He was contemptuous of all those people who thought there was only one way to live, who wanted to pin a person down with a mortgage and payments on a car and three levels of taxes and four kinds of insurance and lifelong responsibility for a wife and a couple of bratty kids.

Palmer had long since sloughed off wife and kids. It had been easy, like dumping kittens from a car window.

CHAPTER 15

> *I danced with the scribe and the pharisee,*
> *But they would not dance*
> *And they would not follow me.*
> "The Lord of the Dance"

T he most annoying thing about the tent city at Harvard's very door was not its seventy-five homeless residents, it was the infection spreading in the student body and among the so-called liberal members of the faculty. Students and professors were flocking to the overpass, bringing along their expensive Arctic camping equipment, demonstrating their sympathy, sleeping out all night under the cold stars.

"It's politically correct, that's why," said Ellery Beaver, Associate Vice-President for Government and Community Affairs, in his office in Massachusetts Hall. "They'll go along with anything dumb, as long as it's in behalf of the retarded, the alcoholic, the criminal, the drug-addicted, the promiscuous."

Ernest Henshaw looked at him nervously. He had been bending over a file drawer, counting the files. "It's too much," he said vaguely. "It's just too much."

"You said a mouthful. It certainly is a bit much. So the question is, do we talk to the ringleader, this guy Nifto, or do we just ignore the whole thing and not give it the cachet of our official notice?"

Henshaw wasn't listening. "All these files," he said, making a sweeping gesture at the four large cabinets in the corner of his office, "it's too much." He walked to the window and stared across the Yard at the bare branches of the

trees around University Hall. It occurred to him how much better they looked now than in the summertime, when they were clothed in tens of thousands of leaves. How many leaves were there really? He could imagine himself next summer, standing on a ladder to count them, one leaf at a time.

Nature was so excessive! But people were even worse. Look at the way the mail poured in! At this time of year there were catalogues in the mail every day. And then his wife ransacked the catalogues and called an 800 number and used her credit card to order things. And the UPS truck came, and came again, and delivered things in boxes, and the boxes piled up in the back room.

The mountain of boxes was an index of the Henshaws' excess. There were boxes that television sets had come in, and stereos and toasters and tape recorders and clock radios and cordless telephones and microwave ovens and video-cassette recorders and exercise equipment, and all the gee-gaws his wife was so fond of—little tables and footstools and candlesticks and ornaments. The whole house was cluttered with things, the closets bulged with clothing. Sometimes it was difficult to clear the rooms, to shove everything out of the way into the back, the laundry, the toolshed.

Henshaw sometimes felt he was pawing the air, clearing it of boxes. Whenever he walked into the Yard he dared not turn around, because they were trailing after him, a whole baggage train of boxes, tumbling after him, turning end over end, blowing up against the backs of his knees, heaping up behind him.

He nodded at the file cabinets. "Just throw all this stuff out. It's too much."

Ellery Beaver stared at him, murmured, "Right you are," and hurried out of the office.

Something was the matter with the old man. Ellery had been suspicious about the mental condition of his boss before, but now he was sure of it. Ernest Henshaw must have had a stroke or something. He was definitely barmy.

Ellery was right—something had indeed happened to Ernest Henshaw. Of course it was possible that it had been a stroke, but it was also possible that he had been granted a new vision. Perhaps he had been carried aloft to a place high above the world from which he could look down and see it truly for the first time.

Whatever the reason, Ernest Henshaw was a changed man, unable to carry on.

CHAPTER 16

So all you young lasses, stand straight and stand firm,
Keep everything tight and close down,
For if anything happens in forty weeks' time,
The blame will be laid on the clown.
　　　　　　　Traditional British Mummers' Play

Sarah couldn't keep it a secret from Morgan any longer. Her clothes were too tight. She had taken to wearing her biggest shirts and the same old skirt with the elastic waistband. The failure of the baby to thrash out with its arms and legs had become a consuming worry, as though it were a punishment for her secrecy, for not giving Morgan a chance to veto the whole idea while there was still time.

One morning, lying warmly beside him in bed, Sarah decided the moment had come. Although it was nearly seven o'clock, the sky was still dark. The dawnlight of the dark December morning barely distinguished the objects in the room. Her desk was a gray shape, and so was the dresser and the chair with her sweater draped over the back. She could hear a car start up outside. The inhabitants of the street were already going to work.

"Morgan," she murmured, caressing his face, kissing the place where his beard met his bare cheek. "Morgan, darling, listen."

"Darling," repeated Morgan sleepily, reaching out for her, pulling her close.

Her voice was soft, but the words came out plain. "Morgan, we're going to have a baby." She kissed him again. "I'm sorry. I've been pregnant for five months. It's due on April thirteenth. I know I should have told you."

Morgan sat up and looked at her. He was wide awake. "Oh, Sarah, my dear." Tenderly he embraced her. "Of course you should have told me! My poor darling, are you all right?"

Sarah said she was fine, just fine, and in a moment they were making love. Then they lay in each other's arms and murmured about what it would mean to have a baby in the house, how they would manage. They would have to find a bigger place. They would have to move.

Astonished and relieved, Sarah slipped out of bed and brought him the little garment she had bought for the baby. "Look."

Morgan laughed, and fingered the fleecy cloth. His doubts had vanished. His constricted breath was coming freely once again.

"Let's not tell anyone," said Sarah. "Let's wait till the Revels are over. Now, darling, lie down and go back to sleep. I have to hurry. I've got a breakfast meeting with Tom."

Morgan grinned and lay back on the pillow and watched her move around the room getting dressed. Who cared about Tom Cobb now? It was Morgan Bailey who was the father of her child.

When he woke up an hour later Sarah was gone. The room was rosy with morning light. Cars were moving slowly on the street below. Sarah had left a note on the table—

> Darling,
> Meet me at three o'clock?
> I love you.*
>
> Sarah
>
> *Passionately!

Morgan smiled, thinking of the baby. He put the precious note in his desk drawer and made himself a scrappy breakfast.

But as he sat down to eat it, he had a queer thought. Sarah had said the baby was due on April thirteenth. April thirteenth? Then when had it been conceived?

Morgan had a lot to do that day. He wanted to check the cornfield in Concord and take a look at the neighboring ponds. It would take him all morning and afternoon. But now he jumped up from the table and found this year's calendar and the new one for next year.

The gestation period in humans was 280 days. Morgan flipped the pages of the two calendars and counted back from April thirteenth. *Two hundred seventy-eight, two hundred seventy-nine, two hundred eighty*—his finger landed on July first. July first, this year, was when conception must have taken place.

But on July first Morgan had been attending that conference of ornithologists at the College of the Atlantic in Bar Harbor. There it was on the calendar, staring him in the face, a bracket around June thirtieth, July first, and July second, with Sarah's scribbled note, *Morgan in Bar Harbor.*

The pain was physical. Morgan groaned and sank his face in his hands. Furiously he ripped out the calendar page and tore it up and flung the pieces in the wastebasket. Then he ran across the room, snatched up the little garment Sarah had bought for the baby, slashed it with a pair of scissors, and dropped it on the table in plain sight. *Let her see how wretched I am! Let her pity me!*

The violent action comforted him. His pain diminished, and he felt an access of cleverness. The new prickles of intelligence on his scalp began to quiver.

At Niki's Market he wandered up and down the aisles,

looking for the right kind of candy. Niki's catered to the high-school kids from Cambridge Rindge and Latin. It was full of junk food. There they were, the chocolate bars, lined up in a row—Snickers and Milky Ways and Mars Bars and Tastychox. Morgan bought several Tastychox and took them home. Then he got to work on the delicate task of removing the wrappings very, very carefully.

CHAPTER 17

Christmas is coming,
The geese are getting fat,
Please to put a penny
In the old man's hat.
  Traditional nursery rhyme

The days were growing ever shorter, the darkness settling in earlier every afternoon. For the Christmas shoppers in Harvard Square the sparkling store windows brightened the winter gloom.

They were a magnet for Helen Henshaw, especially the clever shops in the Holyoke Center arcade, so full of charming small luxuries, fripperies from all over the world. Helen's favorite was a shop specializing in little snow scenes in glass balls, the kind you shake to make the snow fall. She bought one to show to her favorite client, Margo Beaver, who wanted some sort of collectible for her new bedroom, something she could shop for wherever she traveled, because that would be such fun.

To Arlo Field, Christmas meant a tense holiday with his mother in Pittsfield. Every year he connected the impossible task of finding a present for her with the shriveling of the hours of sunshine.

Yesterday the time between sunrise and sunset had lasted only nine hours and seven minutes. A week from Friday, the shortest day of the year, the sun-starved people of this latitude would enjoy only nine hours and four paltry minutes of daylight.

To Homer Kelly too, the season was bleak. In spite of Homer's normal pathological elation and cross-eyed transcendental rapture, he was at heart a pessimist. The world

was a perpetual glory, humankind an ongoing disappointment. In Homer's judgment Christmas was a frantic scram-
ble to overcome the doldrums of winter.

His wife was optimistic by nature, but this year even
Mary Kelly found the Christmas spirit hard to come by,
that expensive annual befuddlement masquerading as jol-
lity and mirth. Harvard Towers was at fault. The contrast
between the gleeful people shopping in Harvard Square
and the penniless inhabitants of Palmer Nifto's tent city
made a farce out of Christmas.

Mary would have liked to forget people's troubles, she
would have preferred not to think about homelessness and
poverty, she had meant to gather around her the fantasy
and ringing bells of the Christmas season. After all, that
was why she had joined the Revels in the first place—to
deck the halls with boughs of holly, to rejoice in a Christian fantasy about a miraculous birth, to believe for a week
or two in angels and a shining star.

But the festive illusion, thinly maintained inside Memorial Hall, was utterly destroyed outside the building by
the cluster of tents on the overpass, by Emily Pollock with
her shrill voice on the open mike, by the Portapotties, by
the humped shape of Maggody in his blankets and the
cacophony of Vergil Taylor's ghetto blaster, and by the in-
scrutable dark glasses of Palmer Nifto.

Coming out of an afternoon rehearsal into the December
dark, Mary walked around Memorial Hall to see what was
going on.

The Hari Krishna kids were there, dancing and clash-
ing their cymbals, rocking back and forth on their big
sneakers, chanting something or other, their saffron
robes swaying over their heavy sweaters. Linda Bunting's
kids hopped up and down, clapping their hands, and Bob

Chumley's dogs pranced on their hind legs and barked. Emily Pollock was there too, twirling and gyrating with the Hari Krishna, twisting her hands to make her bangles jingle. A woman in a purple hat caught at Mary's arm, and pontificated on the worship of Krishna as a sacred milkman.

"Did you know," said Dr. Box, "that Krishna refused to worship the solar image? *I am a God,* he said, *so why should I salute the sun?*"

"A classic case of hubris," said Mary, shaking her head wisely. "A very dangerous attitude." Escaping from Dr. Box, she dodged past her to the central patch of grass, where a bunch of jolly students had set up a Christmas tree. They were draping it with lights and singing "O Little Town of Bethlehem."

Their light voices clashed with the chant of the Hari Krishna, but it didn't matter. The more noise the better. The churchwomen behind the food table smiled as they served hot soup in paper cups, ladling it out of hot pots plugged into Palmer Nifto's immense network of extension cords.

"Oh!" cried everyone as the lights on the Christmas tree went on. Then—*ppppfffft*—there was a small explosion, and the lights went out.

There were gasps, then laughter. Inside his command headquarters Palmer Nifto swore as his computer went down. In all the tents the electric heaters faded to black. The Hari Krishna people stopped singing, then gamely started up again in the dark.

For a moment Mary Kelly had the insane idea that Dr. Box's blasphemy against the sun had blacked out all the lights. Then she tried to think what to do, because it was obvious that these people couldn't sleep out-of-doors

without heat. Looking around at the jumble of dark lump-
ish dwellings and the thick silhouettes of men, women,
and children wrapped up against the cold, she saw them
once again as a medieval village struggling to endure the
winter while the mistral blew from the Alps, and snow
piled up to the rooftops, and the wind shrieked across a
thousand miles of Siberian steppe.

Her first impulse was to shout, *Make the sun come back!*
Bang on kettles! Bang on pots! Her second was to call out,
"Gretchen! Has anybody seen Gretchen?"

But Gretchen was half a mile away, far from the di-
shevelment of Harvard Towers with its blown fuses, far
away beyond the cold grass of Cambridge Common and
the heavy traffic on Massachusetts Avenue and Garden
Street.

Gretchen was experiencing the Christmas season
among the beautiful houses on Brattle Street. She was not
aware that Thomas Brattle had corresponded with Isaac
Newton; she didn't know that George Washington had
lived here, and Henry Wadsworth Longfellow. She saw
only the splendid picket fences and the great arks of
houses, their windows glowing softly. If there was
wretchedness inside those walls, Gretchen did not know
it. If suicidal sons and anorexic daughters, alcoholic mothers and unemployed fathers lived on Brattle Street, it was
unsuspected by Gretchen Milligan. She saw only the glim-
mer of lighted Christmas trees, and imagined the happy
families within.

Heavy as she was with a baby about to be born,
Gretchen was wearied by her long walk. But she pushed
on to the Divinity School and found her secret passage to
Berkeley Street.

Yes, here was the place she loved best. Gretchen

stopped and leaned against the fence to stare. The house looked lovelier than ever, with electric candles in the windows and a wreath on the wall of the front porch. If the Cambridge City Council were to say to her, "Gretchen Milligan, this document grants you ownership of any property in the city—take your pick," she would choose this house on Berkeley Street with its yellow clapboards and tall windows and pretty trees.

From behind the fence Gretchen inspected all the windows in turn, hoping to see the mistress of the house. Sometimes she was visible, striding quickly from room to room, a handsome woman, smartly dressed—but today she was nowhere to be seen. Gretchen walked boldly up the driveway, hoping to see her through the kitchen win-

dow, but the woman remained out of sight. Gretchen began moving around to the back.

"May I help you?"

Someone was standing on the porch. It was the master
of the house. Indoors he appeared to be a slow-moving
man with gray hair and glasses, but outside he seemed
different—taller, balder, paler. He was looking at her
strangely.

"Oh, no thanks," said Gretchen. "I was just—I mean, I
just moved in down the street. I got mixed up. I thought
this was my house."

"Oh?" the man said gently. "Which house is your
house?"

"Oh, wow, like I forget the number. You see, I'm so
new." Gretchen laughed, and started back down the driveway. "Well, I'm glad to meet my new neighbor. We'll be
seeing each other often, I'll bet. *Ciao!*"

The owner of the house stared after the odd-looking
pregnant girl with the freckled face and bushy hair. He
guessed she was homeless, because he had seen her on JFK
Street pushing a grocery cart full of her stuff.

Ernest Henshaw went back indoors and hurried to the
living room at the front of the house. Edging through a
clutter of small tables covered with brass ornaments, he
moved to the window to watch Gretchen's retreat.

Longing sprang up in his heart.

CHAPTER 18

I am the dragon, here are my jaws!
I am the dragon, here are my claws!
Saint George and the Dragon

The overloading of the wiring system at Harvard Towers resulted in a general power failure all over Harvard University. When Millie from Phillips Brooks House attached the plug of the Christmas-tree lights to an extension cord connected to a labyrinth of other extension cords already supplying power to twenty-two electric heaters, ten television sets, twenty-five lamps, four hot pots, and Palmer Nifto's computer and fax machine, the effect was catastrophic.

The Director of Buildings and Grounds insisted that it couldn't happen, but it did. Harvard University went black.

There were howls of anguish from men and women all over the university when the terminals of their computers were suddenly extinguished. Classrooms went dark. A slide projector in the Fogg Museum paused in its progress through the history of classical architecture with a flashing glimpse of the ruins of Baalbek. Scholars in the depths of Widener Library had to grope their way out of pitch-black stacks, then find the stairs and ascend flight after flight, to stumble into the dimness of the catalogue room at last with pitiful cries. The babel of language instruction in the earphones of students in the basement of Boylston Hall was cut off in mid-syllable. The power tools of workmen rehabbing the Lowell Lecture Hall went dead. The electron microscopes in the Gordon McKay Physics Lab fizzled out. The centrifuges splicing one gene to another stopped working, and a billion genes milled around in confusion. Heat leaked out of all the buildings as the oil feed to a hundred furnaces lost power. The new clocks on the tower of Memorial Hall stopped cold at four-forty-eight. A couple of security guards from the Harvard Police Department rushed off to dormitories in the Radcliffe Yard with batteries for the newfangled locks on the doors, to keep the electronic card keys working.

Only in Harvard Divinity School's Andover Hall did work go on as before. Bundles of candles from the second-floor chapel were passed from hand to hand, and people began moving through the halls like medieval monks.

When the lights went out in Sanders Theatre, Arlo Field was rehearsing the part of Saint George, lying on the floor of the stage playing dead. As the cry went up, "Power's out," he leaped to his feet.

"It's out all over," reported Kevin Barnes.

"Jesus," said Arlo to Tom Cobb, "my camera, the timing will be thrown off." He looked at his watch, couldn't see it, and held it up to the light from the windows above the mezzanine, which were glimmering with the flicker of headlights moving along Quincy Street. The watch said four-forty-eight. Arlo tore off his Red Cross tunic and jumped off the stage.

"Hey," said Homer, who was curious about Arlo's camera, "can I come?" He looked at Sarah. "Is it okay? Are we through for the day?"

"Oh, well, hell," said Tom Cobb, "we might as well quit."

"Great," said Jeffery Peck, one of the other Morris dancers. "Let's get out of here."

Arlo looked at Sarah in the dim light and said boldly,

"Would you like to come too? There's a great view up there."

"Oh, yes," said Sarah, "yes, I would." She seemed pleased. But then, to Arlo's chagrin, Kevin, Tom, and Jeff volunteered to come along.

They poured out of the north door of Memorial Hall and headed across the street. The stepped pyramid of the Science Center, normally so brilliant with lighted class-rooms and laboratories, was completely dark. Beyond it, blacked-out buildings stretched along Oxford Street as far as the eye could see.

"Oh, God, I forgot," said Arlo, "we'll have to climb the stairs to the eighth floor. The elevators won't be working." He glanced at Sarah. "Do you mind climbing all that way?"

"Of course not." Sarah linked arms with Homer on one side and Tom on the other. *Come on, baby, this will shake you up.*

"Wait, Sarah!" Someone was running after them, shouting.

"Why, Morgan," said Sarah, "what are you doing here?"

"I just thought I'd come to meet you," said Morgan defensively. "Anything wrong with that?"

Sarah hurried back to him and took his arm and squeezed it. "Of course not. Come on. Arlo's going to show us something on the eighth floor."

"But what happened?" said Morgan. "Why is everything so dark?"

"Nobody knows," said Tom Cobb. "Everything went kapoof."

Homer waved his arms and explained the whole thing. "Somebody threw this huge enormous switch labeled *Main Fuse, Harvard University.* It must be some diabolical anti-intellectual plot, the end of higher education as we know it."

They climbed the steps to the east door of the Science Center. Within the glass walls flashlights fumbled in the dark.

Jeffery Peck glanced back at Morgan and Sarah. "Funny guy," he said to Arlo.

"Famous ornithologist," said Arlo.

"No kidding? Funny guy just the same."

"Sarah," whispered Morgan, "you shouldn't be climbing a lot of stairs, not now."

"Oh, don't worry," said Sarah. "I'll take it easy."

But all of them were worn out by the time they reached Arlo's lab on the eighth floor.

"Oh, hey, hi there." Giggling, Chickie Pickett loomed out of the shadows. Chickie knew almost everybody, even in the dark. "Hi, Arlo; hi, Morgan; hi, Sarah." Morgan was surprised to discover that Chickie even knew Kevin Barnes. In fact, he was putting his arms around her. She must know him very well indeed. "Oh, hey, Arlo," said Chickie, disentangling herself from Kevin, "the camera clock's stopped. And, wow, like I forgot to notice the time."

"It's okay," said Arlo, "I looked at my watch. The power went off at four-forty-eight. I hope to God it comes on again soon. There's only one more exposure before the shortest day."

Kevin and Chickie withdrew to the far side of the room to whisper in the corner. Chickie was shivering in a skintight athletic suit. Morgan watched enviously as Kevin wrapped his jacket around her.

Sarah wanted to know what Arlo's camera was for, what it was that he did up here, what his work was all about. Arlo explained about the analemma in a couple of sentences. Homer didn't understand, and he asked questions. Sarah said, "Oh, right, but—" Morgan was silent, Chickie squealed from the back of the room, and Tom Cobb opened the door and went out on the terrace.

They followed him, and everybody gasped at the view.

"Great place you've got up here," said Tom, looking southwest at Harvard Square, glowing brightly beyond the dark blotch that was the university. Below them the tents of Harvard Towers glimmered from within with fiery sources of light.

Arlo and Homer leaned over the railing to the west and looked out over Cambridge Common. "Is it true you used to be a policeman?" said Arlo, who had heard a rumor somewhere. "A traffic cop?"

"Well, yes, for a while. Then I investigated homicides for the District Attorney of Middlesex County."

"Homicides, no kidding! Did you catch any murderers?"

"One or two," admitted Homer, puffed up with false modesty.

Tom moved to the east side of the terrace and looked beyond the dark bulk of Memorial Hall. "My God, you can see all of Boston from here."

Morgan stood next to him and craned his neck over the railing to look at the courtyard far below. Directly below them was the glass roof of the Greenhouse cafeteria. *If you dropped something, it would fall a long way down.*

Drawing closer, he slipped something into the pocket of Tom's padded parka.

PART THREE

THE HERO COMBAT

TURKEY SNIPE
Battle, battle, battle I will call,
And see which on the ground shall fall.

KING GEORGE
Battle, battle, I will cry,
To see which on the ground shall lie.

Traditional British Mummers' Play

CHAPTER 19

In comes I, Old Beelzebub
Over my shoulder I carries my club,
In my hand a dripping pan,
Don't you think I'm a jolly old man?
      Traditional British Mummers' Play

The power outage at Harvard University lasted only a few hours.

Donald Maderna, mechanical foreman for the North Yard, listened with relief to the dull rumble of the furnace in the basement of the Science Center. "How the hell did it happen anyhow?"

"God knows," said the building manager.

On the eighth floor Arlo Field scribbled *8:14 p.m.* in his notebook and set to work at once to adjust the timer on his camera.

A lost scholar in Widener Library who had snuggled down on the floor and gone to sleep next to the bottom shelf of Indochinese folklore on Level D of the stacks, woke up as the lightbulb over his head turned on. Deep down in the center of the earth he was perfectly warm. He staggered to his feet, turned off the light switch, and lay down again, his head pillowed on the 1938 volume of the *Journal of the Siam Society*. Shutting his eyes, he went back to sleep.

"I thought I told you these electrical connections are illegal," said Sumner Plover, glaring at Palmer Nifto with his arms folded on his chest. Behind Sumner stood three more officers of the Harvard Police Department, glowering fiercely at Palmer.

"Do you expect us to freeze to death?" said Palmer piteously. He glanced around for bulging Gretchen, but she was nowhere in sight. "Linda," he shouted. But Linda Bunting was enfolded between her children in her tent, and she wasn't about to get up.

"Disconnect everything," commanded Sumner.

At once the four officers began jerking at extension cords, moving from tent to tent, commandeering electric heaters, microwave ovens, and toasters, while Palmer protested loudly, "Those appliances are private property. You are condemning us to death. There are small children here, mothers-to-be, helpless elderly men and women."

"You should have thought of that before bringing them here," said Sumner, doing his best to stand up to Palmer Nifto, who always had the best lines. "Come on, you people," he bawled, "it's a cold night. We've got a bus to take you to the shelter at University Lutheran. Everybody out!"

They went—Emily Pollock, old man Maggody, Guthrie Jones, Linda Bunting and her two children, and all the rest—all but Bob Chumley and his dogs.

"It's a two-dog night," said Bob, grinning at the Harvard cop who looked into his tent. "We'll be okay. Uny Lu wouldn't take the three of us anyway."

Sumner Plover gaped. "Uny Lu?"

"University Lutheran," murmured Bob, burrowing back down between his dogs.

When Gretchen came back from Berkeley Street, everybody but Bob had been picked up. Mary and Homer Kelly had been looking for her. They swept her up and drove her to Bright Day House in Somerville, where she was welcomed with hugs and scoldings.

"What's your due date, dear?" said the counselor, looking at her swollen tummy. "It must be pretty soon."

"Oh, God, it was last week," said Gretchen. "I'm overdue. The kid's really jumping around in there. Feel it."

The counselor put her hand on Gretchen's abdomen. "It's knocking on the door, all right. Now, Gretchen, you are not to budge from this house again, do you hear me?"

"Okay," said Gretchen, but she didn't mean it.

As for Palmer Nifto, shelters were not for him. Palmer had spent too many winter nights in the Pine Street Inn, where five hundred people were crowded in on top of one another, where there was no privacy, where some of the men were violent and some were crazies who shouted all night.

He had found a corner of Memorial Hall that was toasty and warm. It was the office of the director, right off the balcony above the great hall. There were stained-glass windows, a wall-to-wall carpet, a comfortable sofa, and the latest thing in telephones. Visiting the office one day on a phony errand, Palmer had stuffed a tiny piece of paper into the hole in the doorjamb. The latch clicked, but the door remained unlocked.

Tonight the telephone came in handy. Lounging on the sofa with the phone nestled on his shoulder, Palmer outfoxed Sumner Plover.

Next day he was back at Harvard Towers, beckoning to another truck. This one carried a very large and ugly machine. It was a secondhand generator, contributed by a neighbor on Francis Avenue, a professor of immense distinction who kept it in his garage. "Good, good," shouted Palmer, walking in front of the truck. "A little more, a little more, okay, stop."

The truck driver got out and climbed up on the back and wrestled with the generator. "Okay, now," he said, "are you ready? I'll throw in the clutch."

At once there was a loud whining noise, and a steady supply of electric current passed through the field coils to support the new collection of electric heaters that had appeared out of nowhere as if by magic.

The whole citizenry of Harvard Towers was back. Even Gretchen Milligan, ever loyal to the cause, stole out of Bright Day to display her bulging figure to the world in the cause of justice and mercy and housing for the homeless.

Officer Plover was outraged. Looking up at the humming generator on the back of the truck, he said, "Where did you get that?"

Palmer uttered the prestigious name, and Sumner Plover blanched. "Well, you can't have it here," he said lamely.

"Why not?" said Palmer. "We're not borrowing one single ampere of electricity from the sacred power supply of Harvard University."

Sumner was stymied. He changed the subject. "You asked for a meeting with Vice-President Henshaw? Well, it's been arranged. He can see you this afternoon at three-thirty. It's the only time available for the next three weeks, so you'd better be on time."

Palmer smiled, and inspected his dirty fingernails. Flicking back his grubby cuff, he examined his watch, a fine specimen lifted from the wrist of a sleeping druggie in Central Square. It told the time in Rio, London, and Katmandu. "I'll see what I can do," he said loftily. "My own schedule is pretty full."

But of course Palmer appeared in Henshaw's office in Massachusetts Hall that afternoon, and only fifteen minutes late—an interval calculated to irritate Vice-President Henshaw without enraging him to the point of canceling the meeting.

It turned out that it was the Associate Vice-President who did most of the talking. Henshaw was in the room, but he said very little.

"You cannot deny," said Nifto, jumping in with both feet, "the moral responsibility of this institution for the plight of the homeless people of Cambridge. Harvard University owns real estate all over the city. You have an endowment of six billion dollars. Surely some small fraction of your holdings would house all the homeless mothers, pregnant teenagers, and helpless old men at your very gates, people who are at this moment without shelter in the middle of winter?"

The interview was the strangest encounter of Ellery Beaver's career. "My dear Mr. Nifto," he said smoothly, glancing at his boss, who was gazing at the rug, "I believe the university is already doing a great deal for the homeless people of Cambridge. The students of Phillips Brooks House, just as one example, are the sole staff of the shelter at University Lutheran. It is the active expression of their spiritual life. They also—"

"Oh, right," said Palmer Nifto, "you mean Scottie and Brad and Millie, oh, sure, we're old buddies. But I'm talking about empowerment here. What precisely is the university going to do to supply permanent housing for the ninety-seven homeless people encamped on the overpass beside Harvard Yard during the Christmas season? I assure you, we are not going away."

"If you are trespassing on our property," said Ellery Beaver with a touch of menace in his voice, "I believe we can make you go away."

"Your property?" said Palmer, leaping to take advantage. "I understand your ownership of the property is debatable. You can make us go away? Drag us out? We'll have cameras there from Channel Four so fast it'll knock your socks off. You might be interested to know that we're negotiating with the network right now for joint sponsorship of a stadium appearance by Paul Newman and Joanne Woodward."

This was a lie, but it gave Ellery Beaver a shock. There was a pause, into which Vice-President Henshaw inserted an odd question. "Tell me, Mr. Nifto, your tents, are they empty?"

"Empty?"

"I mean, you don't have curtains and pillows in your tents?"

"Curtains? Well, no, of course we don't have curtains. Tents don't have, like windows."

This dialogue was certainly bizarre, and yet Ernest Henshaw and Palmer Nifto might have had something to say to each other if Ellery Beaver had been somewhere else. Both were alienated from a world gone mad. The only difference between them was that Henshaw turned away with horror and revulsion, while Nifto hurled every stick and stone that came into his hand.

Ellery Beaver broke in, trying to get the conversation back on track.

"Well, of course we're not going to evict you. We want to talk. We want to look at your problem from all sides. As I understand it, homelessness has many causes, both social and economic. We want to organize a symposium. We want you to conduct a seminar during the reading period, 'Homelessness and the Urban Condition,' something of that sort. But of course we would expect you and your friends to leave the premises first. We cannot talk under pressure."

Palmer was wary. "I heard you guys would do this, try to talk us to death. I mean, like there was a tent city at the Massachusetts Institute of Technology, and the establishment wouldn't talk, they moved in with bulldozers and mashed everything down. But at least they were honest. What the hell good does it do to talk?"

Ellery Beaver laughed loudly. "Oh, MIT, they wouldn't have a clue. You people scared them out of their wits. But I assure you, this is a different sort of institution. We really care. We want to hear your ideas, your whole philosophical position, how you hope to relate to the city, the

church, the university. Of course, you understand that we can do nothing inconsistent with the primary educational purposes of the university."

"The point is," said Palmer coldly, "talking is all very well, but what happens after that? Like I was thinking, they're repairing this building on Kirkland Street. Why don't you turn it over to us? Fix it up with, you know, apartments? We move in, we don't bother you any more."

Ellery Beaver's ruddy face turned pale. He flicked a glance at Henshaw, whose stillness was the stillness of death. "You mean," he said, stuttering, "Lowell Lecture Hall?"

"Yes, that's the one. Like it's got a lot of columns and pediments, right? It would do just fine. Get us off your back."

"But, my God, Lowell Lecture Hall!"

Then Vice-President Henshaw raised his eyes at last, and spoke up. "What about armoires? Have you people got any armoires?"

Ellery Beaver looked away, embarrassed, but Palmer turned his head and looked squarely at Ernest Henshaw for the first time.

The man had a narrow face, a small nose, large round glasses, tiny ears, a high balding forehead, and gray hair cut short against his skull. His suit was gray, his Oxford-cloth shirt was blue as the summer sky, his necktie was patterned with tennis racquets. His shoes were brown and shining, his socks showed no speck of bare white leg. He was the perfect Harvard alumnus of the class of thirty years back—except for his eyes.

Henshaw's eyes were very small in their narrow slits. They glittered directly at Palmer Nifto, and he could see that they were insane.

CHAPTER 20

Down in yon forest there stands a hall:
The bells of paradise I heard them ring:
It's cover'd all over with purple and pall:
And I love my Lord Jesus above anything.

In that hall there stands a bed:
The bells of paradise I heard them ring:
It's cover'd all over with scarlet so red:
And I love my Lord Jesus above anything.

Under that bed there runs a flood:
The bells of paradise I heard them ring:
The one half runs water, the other runs blood:
And I love my Lord Jesus above anything.

Carol from *Richard Hill's Commonplace Book,*
circa 1500

The things that were going on inside and outside Memorial Hall had begun to intertwine.

In Sanders Theatre the back rows of benches were often occupied by people who leaked out of the tent city to get warm, then stayed to watch the succession of dramatic episodes on the stage.

And the Revels performers had begun to take an interest in the tent city. At lunchtime on Saturday the Morris men bounded around outdoors in heavy jackets, stamping on the yellow grass. The men and women of the chorus gathered beside Palmer Nifto's command center and sang "Masters in This Hall" and "Go, Tell It on the Mountain," and then they led everybody in "Silent Night" and "O Come, All Ye Faithful."

Mary Kelly watched the tired gray faces light up as the residents of Harvard Towers sang the familiar words.

They must have learned them as children when they were living in houses. The contrast between the solid walls of the past and the flimsy fabric of the present must surely be painful, but they were all smiling and laughing. Camping here out-of-doors, homeless and lacking in everything, they were experiencing Christmas, however pale and second-class.

Tom Cobb stood beside Mary, applauding. "It's a damn shame," he said. "Why doesn't somebody do something about it?"

"About homelessness?" said Mary. "Oh, right." She had heard the same thing so many times, she had said it herself so often, what good did it do to talk?

But Tom Cobb was in a talkative mood. Tom was a recently divorced estate attorney with a lucrative practice. He was Sarah Bailey's right-hand man, and the best dancer among the Morris men. When the six of them were stamping around on the stage, Mary always kept her eyes on Tom, because he was so lithe and strong and graceful, leaping higher than the rest. Everyone liked Tom Cobb. He was jocular and cheerful, a practical jokester with a corny sense of humor. His jokes were awful and made everybody groan, but they laughed at the same time. His world seemed so sunny and easy-going. Why wasn't it the true one, why wasn't everyone like Tom?

Even the homeless people liked him, although his simple-minded optimism had no solution to their predicament, only the superficial question *Why doesn't somebody do something?*—which was no answer at all.

They were singing again, "The First Noel." "Have a choc?" said Tom, holding out a candy bar to Mary.

"Oh, no, thanks. I just had a couple of doughnuts."

"Well, okay." Tom bit off a big chunk. "Uh-oh, lunch break's over. Here comes Sarah."

Sarah Bailey had come out to urge everyone back inside, but at once she noticed Gretchen Milligan in the circle of homeless people. She couldn't help wondering if she herself would ever be as big as that.

Fascinated, she approached Gretchen and struck up a conversation. "When's your baby due?"

"Oh, Jesus, it was due last week."

"Is somebody looking after you? Shouldn't you be in the hospital?"

"Oh, God, no. When the time comes I'll go to Saint Elizabeth's. Jesus, I'm supposed to be at Bright Day right now. It's this place in Somerville."

Sarah couldn't control her curiosity. "Do you feel all right? Is the baby—you know, is it active?"

"Active!" Gretchen put her hands on her stomach. "My God, it's playing hockey in there. Feel it, go ahead, feel it."

Timidly Sarah put one hand on Gretchen's big round ball. Yes, through her fingers came a thump and a restless drumming. Trembling, she dropped her hand, full of envy. She couldn't help seeing this very young girl as a matriarch with hordes of children and grandchildren around her knees. She felt like crying.

But rehearsal time was growing short. Sarah pulled herself together and shouted at everybody to come back inside.

Homer Kelly had put on his giant's mask for the first time. It was huge, with a shaggy mop of hair, fierce eyes, and a mouth full of sharp teeth. He had spent all morning waiting around in the great hall, terrifying the children, running at them with loud roars while they scuttled away screaming and giggling. He had taken off the mask to eat lunch, and it still wasn't time to go onstage, roaring and raking the air with his claws.

He was bored. He stood waiting on the steps at the back of the stage while the Morris men went through their paces, gracefully, twirling their handkerchiefs and waggling their legs.

He was sick and tired of waiting. He wanted to drive home with Mary and look at the water level in the furnace. He hadn't checked it lately, and it was probably low. What if the cutoff didn't work? The furnace would start heating up, and then—Christ!—what would happen after that? There were more damned problems connected with domestic life in a New England winter. "Fee-fi-fo-fum," he grumbled under his breath, swinging his club.

At last Tom signaled the final measures of the dance. The concertina tiddled the end of the tune, and all twelve feet crashed down and stood still.

"Wonderful," said Walt.

Homer flattened himself against the railing to allow the Morris men to tramp offstage. But, oh, God, they weren't finished after all, they were picking up their swords, they were going to do an entirely different dance. Jesus, this could go on all afternoon.

He shifted his weight from one leg to the other, and pulled his mask up on the top of his head. Now they were stopping again. A sword clattered to the floor. What the hell was the matter this time?

"Tom, are you all right?" Sarah ran up the stairs at the front of the stage. Everyone was looking at one of the dancers, who was doubled over, clutching himself around the middle.

"Oh, God," groaned Tom Cobb. He fell to his knees.

Sarah knelt beside him. "Tom, Tom, where does it hurt?"

Tom gasped through clenched teeth. "Christ, it's not my appendix. They already took it out." He rolled moaning on the floor.

Mary Kelly had been watching him dance, enjoying the way Tom's feet seemed to bound up off the floor, the way he grinned as he twirled his handkerchief and laughed as he executed the figures so gracefully. But now the jolly jokester was pale and panting, his face contorted with pain. He tried to get up and fell back with a scream.

"Quick," said Mary, "Cambridge Hospital. It's just up the street."

Homer Kelly tore off his mask. "Our car's right outside." He picked up Tom by the shoulders and a couple of the dancers took his feet, and somebody covered him with a coat. "Okay," said Homer, "let's get him down the stairs. Gently, gently."

"Oh, don't," groaned Tom, "please don't. Oh, *Christ.*"

They were a hushed and shuffling procession, heading for the north door. Walt hurried ahead to hold it open. Children stared from the entrance to the great hall. Mary ran down the north steps, unlocked the car, and opened the two back doors.

Getting Tom into the back seat was a grim struggle, with Homer pulling on one side and Jeffery Peck pushing on the other, and Tom writhing in the middle. At the emergency entrance to the hospital the experts took over. Homer and Mary and Jeffery watched as Tom was hurried away on a stretcher. They looked at one another silently, and Mary shook her head with a gesture of pity and helplessness.

Tom Cobb died an hour later on the operating table. The anesthetist monitoring his life signs threw up her hands. The surgeon cursed. Then there was no sound but the heaving of the stomach pump.

"Turn the fucking thing off," said the surgeon.

"Pathology?" said the orderly. "Shall I should take him to Pathology?"

"Oh, God, yes. There's no excuse for this. Look at that gooey brown mess! What the hell was he eating?"

CHAPTER 21

Horrible, terrible, what hast thou done?
Thou has killed my only dearly beloved son.
                    Traditional British Mummers' Play

It was the second funeral in Harvard's Memorial Church for Mary and Homer Kelly. They had sat here in the past, a long time ago, grieving for someone they hardly knew. Now it was the turn of Tom Cobb, estate lawyer for Ropes and Gray, Morris dancer, jazz flutist, and one of the stage managers for the Christmas Revels.

The Kellys had known Tom only slightly as Sarah's colleague and as one of the Morris dancers. But Homer felt a savage sympathy for the young man who had tossed in such anguish on the back seat of his car.

And death always hit him hard, whether natural or unnatural. After investigating a number of cold-blooded homicides in his time, Homer had come to the conclusion that the worst kind of human extermination wasn't murder, it was the everyday continuous slaughter of the entire human race. The older he got, the more often some old friend or acquaintance stumbled and fell off the edge of that terrible cliff. You'd think the survivors would get used to it. But Homer never did. He couldn't just glance back in surprise and say, *Whoops, too bad!,* and scuttle on, scrabbling his way along the ever-narrowing path on the mountainside, minding his P's and Q's.

Sitting beside Mary in the warm air of Memorial Church, he wondered if he ought to reveal himself to Sarah Bailey, and tell her about his old credentials as a lieutenant detective in the office of the District Attorney of Middlesex

County. Except for Arlo Field, nobody in the Revels crew knew about his history as a policeman. Well, it didn't matter. Homer had no wish to volunteer his services. After all, the Cambridge Police were looking into the sudden death of Tom Cobb, working hand in glove with the Harvard University Police Department. They could handle it.

But in spite of himself Homer felt nosily inquisitive. Once again he was like a dog sniffing the ground, ears cocked, whiskers vibrating. He turned his head left and right and craned his neck over his shoulder to see who had come to the service for Tom Cobb, wondering who might have had it in for him.

The organ boomed massively behind the choir screen. Mary pulled at Homer's coat sleeve and whispered, "Homer, stop it."

"Stop what?"

"Stop staring."

"Oh, all right." Homer shrugged his shoulders and transferred his gaze to the high ceiling, wondering if the young estate lawyer named Tom Cobb was worthy of all this splendor of liturgical apparatus and classical pomposity, of coffered barrel vault and polished pulpit, of red carpet and Corinthian capital. Well, of course, his family must think so. Here they were, Tom's relatives, being ushered into the front pews—a tearstained mother, various brothers, sisters, aunts, and uncles, and an old grandfather.

Arlo came to the service directly from teaching his freshman class, and found a place in the back of the church—Arlo Field, the resident of Apartment B, 329 Huron Avenue, the solar system, the Milky Way galaxy, the expanding universe. He looked at the pulpit, which was draped with a velvet banner, a piece of ecclesiastical haberdashery. He looked up at the lofty white vault of Memorial

Church and saw beyond it the thinning layers of air, the glaring winter sun, pulsing so mysteriously within, and the gibbous moon, dented like a collapsed beach ball. Folding his arms across his best jacket, he thought about Tom Cobb.

Arlo hadn't known Tom very well, but he had found him amusing, and he had wished, like everyone else whose life intersected with Tom's, that he, Arlo Field, could be more like him, that he could loosen up somehow and make friends so winningly. Was it just a matter of liking people better? People in general? Not picking and choosing? Sarah Bailey was like that. She acted as though everyone was *wonderful, just wonderful.*

Arlo felt himself getting more cynical rather than less, more critical of his fellow human beings than ever. He glanced around at the people in the other pews, looking for Sarah, failing to find her.

The church was nearly full. On the other side of the aisle Mary Kelly recognized Arlo and a lot of other Revels people—members of the chorus, the wardrobe mistress, the technical director, the music director, the backstage crew. She watched as latecomers hurried in, muffled in coats and scarves, taking off their hats—the friends and relatives of an attractive and successful man who had died much too young.

Mary nudged Homer as Morgan and Sarah Bailey sat down on the empty bench in front of them. At once the Baileys moved to the end to make room for more.

The newcomers were some of the other Morris dancers, almost unrecognizable in their churchgoing clothes. Their faces were grave. Sarah smiled at them as they shuffled along the row and sat down, edging apart to ease their big shoulders.

Mary was directly behind Morgan Bailey. Without meaning to, she began totting up the things she had against him, beginning with the oddities surrounding the death of Henry Shady under the wheels of Morgan's Range Rover. There was surely something rotten in Morgan's relation with his wife. Anybody could see that. It didn't take two or three professional degrees to understand what was staring you right in the face.

But this morning Morgan and Sarah seemed a loving couple. Sarah was crying, and Morgan leaned over her with what looked like genuine solicitude. She put her head on his shoulder and he wrapped an arm around her. Mary's suspicions dimmed. She glanced at Homer, feeling foolish. But when the Morris dancers edged along the bench where the Baileys were sitting, her mood changed.

Morgan's changed too. Looking around, he saw Sarah patting the space beside her and beckoning. He frowned. Who was this guy, pushing past the others to sit next to her? Then, to his dismay, he recognized Jeffery Peck.

Jeff was another one of the Morris dancers. Now he would be taking over Tom Cobb's job as codirector with Sarah. She was whispering to him, weeping again, and the goddamn guy was putting his arm around her. His arm collided with Morgan's, and Jeff glanced at him and murmured, "Sorry," but he didn't take his arm away. Morgan withdrew his, and sat rigidly beside his wife, fuming, a tide of misery sweeping over him.

The service began with hymns, prayers, and readings from the Bible. One of Tom's law partners talked about the keenness of his colleague's mind and the compassion of his sympathies. Tom's brother spoke about his good nature, and told a couple of his jokes. There were gulps of tearful laughter. Then behind the choir screen Walt sang

"Come Away to the Skies." The last part of the service was the merry music of the concertina playing the "Upstreet Morris."

The Morris men couldn't bear it. The five men sitting in the row with Morgan and Sarah mopped their eyes.

But Morgan heard none of it. His fear had come back. He had been wrong, wrong all the time. It wasn't Tom Cobb, it was Jeffery Peck. Look at Sarah! She was whispering in his ear, she was patting Jeff's hand. He was shoving his big fucking thigh right up against her, and she was shoving back. *Goddamn you, Sarah!*

Mary Kelly watched with surprise as Morgan Bailey grasped his wife's arm, jerked her to her feet, bundled her past the knees of the Morris men, and hurried her out into the shuffling congregation in the aisle, bumping shoulders, pushing through people who were trying to put on their coats. What was *that* all about?

Morgan and Sarah were the first to leave the church. Outside, the air was clear and sparkling. Morgan inhaled a deep shaky breath, but it did no good. Once again his chest was tight and constricted. Once again he could hardly breathe.

CHAPTER 22

We are six dancers bold, as bold as you can see,
We have come to dance this dance to please the company.
Traditional British Mummers' Play

O nce, in Sarah's childhood, the hot-water boiler in the basement had nearly burst. Her father had raced around the house turning on the faucets, and the boiling water had burst out in torrents of scalding steam. There had been a dangerous smell, a sense of fore-boding, a certainty that something terrible was about to happen.

She felt it now, she could almost sense the same smell. This new death, the sudden collapse of Tom Cobb, it was not merely a repetition of the tragedy of Henry Shady, it was a shuddering in the pipes, a pounding rattle in the ra-diator, a hissing of furious steam.

And of course there was the other thing. Her fear about her motionless child was a dull perpetual ache. Surely something was the matter? The idea of the baby, the over-whelming concept of the person inside her, was crucial to her now. It was so strange, the way she kept thinking of herself as the progenitor of a pyramid of descendants. They had come to seem important, her nonexistent pos-terity. They were looking backward at her from the future, tugging at the hem of her skirt, reminding her they had yet to be born.

And last of all there was Morgan. What was the matter with him? He had seemed all right again. He had been so glad about the baby. But she had come home the very same day to find the ruined little garment on the table, slashed to ribbons—what a hideous, wild thing for Morgan to do, what a crude and horrible thing. How he must hate the baby!

If it were really dead, thought Sarah mournfully, it might be the best thing after all.

On the day after Tom's funeral, Sarah sat at the breakfast table across from Morgan, saying little, unable to mention the things that needed to be said. She sipped her coffee and looked at the front page of the *Cambridge Chronicle*, where there was a column about Tom Cobb's death, an interview with the police.

"Look," she said, holding up the paper, "they've been talking with the Cambridge Medical Examiner." She read his opinion aloud. *"A toxic substance is thought to have been the culprit in Cobb's death, but whether administered accidentally or with malicious intent has not been determined."* Sarah put the paper down. "I just don't understand it. Why would anybody hurt a wonderful guy like Tom? Everybody loved Tom." Sarah's eyes filled, but she shook her head and jumped up from the table. "I've got to get busy. We have to recruit another Morris dancer."

Morgan looked at her with his stony face. "I'll do it. I'll take his place."

"You'll do it!" Sarah couldn't believe it. "But, Morgan, you've never tried Morris dancing."

"I'll learn."

Sarah looked at him thoughtfully. "Well, it's true, you're a really good dancer." She turned away briskly. "I'll speak to Jeff."

And when she asked Jeffery Peck, he threw up his hands and said, "Why the hell not?" Jeff had been one of the Morris dancers from the beginning, but he had never before been a stage director, he had never been responsible for whipping a performance into shape. It was a frightening responsibility. Already he was suffering from pre-performance despair. The thing didn't hang together, part didn't follow part, people were never ready to come on when their turns came, and when they did, they just stood there looking at him. Half the little kids were sick. And now the best of the Morris dancers had died horribly, right in front of his eyes.

At this point Jeff didn't give a damn about the performance. They would blunder through somehow or other. Sarah would tie the loose ends together. Sooner or later, thank God, the whole damn thing would be over, and he'd be off to the Virgin Islands. In the meantime he'd carry on with rehearsals and patch together whatever edges Sarah gave him to work on.

But when Morgan Bailey appeared at the next rehearsal, ready to go, Jesus, it was the last straw. Jeff hated taking the time to break him in. Fortunately, the guy learned fast. Sarah's confidence in her husband was justified. Morgan learned the figures quickly, and at leaping and stamping he was a phenomenon. "Step, hop, step, hop, step!" cried Jeff. "In place, singles! Back up, doubles!"

Mary Kelly sat in the back row, looking on, keeping an eye on Morgan. His wretchedness was apparent as he danced, it was visible in his vacant face, in the way he kept glancing at Sarah. Mary was not entirely without sympathy for the poor klutz. She had felt the same misery herself, a few years back, when Homer had been a little too friendly with one of the teaching assistants. When she had burst out with her feelings and accused him, Homer had been flabbergasted, and she had understood at once that a transcendentalist in a state of continuous effervescent euphoria could not be blamed for admiring one of nature's wonders. "I don't want to go to bed with her," explained Homer. "I just want to look at her." And Mary had laughed, her jealousy extinct.

But Morgan's case was different. His torment seemed unending. Any fool could see the misery choked up inside him.

Mary leaned back and watched the stick dance. She liked the noise, the simultaneous thunder of stamping feet. Here there was none of the sinuous perfection of other sorts of dancing. It was a display of old-fashioned masculine strength. It was like fighting, a substitute for battle. The crack of stick against stick echoed the clash of spear against shield, and when they danced with swords in their hands, it was like Carthage and Agincourt and Waterloo.

Morgan was catching on. He was a natural. His leaping was wild and high, it had an animal ferocity and grace. The pounding of his stick against Jeff's was like the clash of horns in a mating battle between two stags. It reminded Mary of a film she had seen. She had been awed by the headlong power of the attack, the primitive, wild lunging, the ringing crash of antler against antler.

Morgan was like the stags. In the dancing of the other five men, the wildness was restrained, it was a response to the rhythmic beat of the concertina. But in Morgan something stronger was letting itself go. There was a savage power in his leaping, barely under control.

The merry music stopped. The six men lowered their sticks, breathing hard. "Bravo, the new man," said one of them, clapping Morgan on the back.

Jeffery Peck said nothing. He was gasping, wiping his forehead, looking at Morgan Bailey. Mary suspected that Morgan had struck Jeff's stick with too much violence, as though he were the enemy in a genuine battle.

Sarah seemed to have no such painful suspicions. She clapped her hands. "Oh, Morgan, that was marvelous. Now, do you think you can handle a sword?"

But in the sword dancing Morgan made a mistake almost at once, missing the first step-back-step. "No, that's wrong," shouted Jeffery.

They all stopped marching in a thundering circle and looked at Morgan. "Sorry," he said, wiping his forehead. "Try again."

This time he was perfect. He had memorized the patterns, he needed only a little prompting, a hoarse whisper, a nudge. The swords flashed blue and clattered against one another as the six men marched in a circle. It was a complicated dance. The men wove in and out, and their swords wove in and out, until at last they interlaced and Jeffery lifted the locked swords high in a miraculous six-sided star. There were whistles of approval from the tech table, while the concertina continued its jolly music, and the six men went on tramping around and around.

"All right, Saint George," cried Sarah, "slip into the middle. Ready? *Now!*"

Arlo Field dodged into the circle, and the men marched around him heavily, their feet pounding on the floor. He stood still, the silent axis of the turning wheel, as Jeff lowered the locked swords over his head. The pace increased, with each man reaching out to grasp the projecting handle of a sword, and then—*snick!*—on a single beat they pulled them out and held them high, and Arlo dropped to the floor. The dancers fell back, as though mortified at what they had done.

Again Sarah clapped her hands. "Arlo, that was perfect. Good for you, Morgan."

"Oh, ow," said Arlo, lifting his head from the floor and

rubbing his neck. "Could you guys be a little more careful next time? Jesus!"

"Oh, sorry," said Jeff.

The children came running in. "No, no, not now," cried Sarah. She laughed and swung one of the little girls high over her head. "All you dancers can go home now. Where's the Doctor? We've got to bring Saint George back to life, or spring will never come. Is there a Doctor in the house?"

A bank teller named Arthur Kline had the part of the Doctor. He sprang up on the stage, put on his top hat, and bounded up to Arlo, who obligingly lay back and pretended to be dead.

"Which end is which?" said the Doctor in mock bewilderment. Bowing over Arlo's feet, he said, "Stick out your tongue."

The Morris dancers had been released. They walked off the stage in procession into the high windy spaces of the memorial corridor—Jeff Peck, Bill Foose, Bernard Fox, Jim Yung, Dan Cone, and Morgan Bailey. Morgan was surprised to see a cherry tree lounging at the north end of the corridor, one of its branches holding a cigarette. He was further surprised to see Chickie Pickett come in from outside, a small luscious figure in a short skirt, her plump legs delectable in black pantyhose.

Morgan started forward, but the cherry tree was ahead of him, throwing its branches around Chickie. Squealing her Betty Boop squeal, she allowed herself to be engulfed.

The morning shift of departing Revelers milled around in the corridor with those arriving for the afternoon rehearsal. Lunchbags came out of knapsacks. There was a fragrance of tunafish and peanut butter. The north and south doors opened and shut, letting in streaks of sunshine and blasts of cold air. No one paid any attention to the guy in dark glasses who was holing up in the telephone booth.

It was Palmer Nifto. "Hello, is this the Furniture Bank? Oh, hi there. I'm looking for sofas. How's your supply today?"

"Sofas?" said the woman at the Furniture Bank. "Hey, have we got sofas. What kind do you want?"

"I don't care what kind. Any old kind. But I need a lot of sofas."

"Consider them yours. What's this for, your tent city? Sure, we've got sixteen, seventeen sofas. Like people buy one of those big white sectionals, and pretty soon it's filthy, and the dog pees on it and the cat throws up, and it looks horrible, so they give it to us and then they go out and buy another sofa. Terrible extravagance. But, listen, like we're overstuffed with sofas. Get 'em off our hands. There's no room for anything else. Shall I send a truck? You want all seventeen sofas?"

"You bet I do," said Palmer Nifto. "I've got this little plan."

In come I, the royal Duke of Northumberland
With my broad sword in my hand.
Where's the man that dares to bid me stand?
I would cut him as small as flies
And send him to the cookshop to make mince-pies.
Traditional British Mummers' Play

It was an emergency meeting in University Hall, in the office of the Dean of the Faculty of Arts and Sciences. The sun poured in through Bulfinch's handsome windows, Copley's portraits of Mr. and Mrs. Nathaniel Appleton looked out from the wall, and the Simon Willard clock over the mantel made a gentle sound, *tock, tick, tock.*

"It's ridiculous," said the Dean. "You mean to say we can't get rid of a bunch of squatters on Harvard property?"

"The question is," explained Ellery Beaver, "whose property is it, really? Does the overpass belong to the university or the city of Cambridge? Remember Mayor Vellucci? He used to bring it up all the time. He claimed it belonged to the city."

The General Counsel made a note. "I'll look into the matter. If it doesn't belong to us, then it's not our problem. Let the Cambridge City Council deal with it." He rocked back in his chair and brought up an amusing technicality. "It seems that the original charter for Memorial Hall forbids any other structure on the Delta—you know, the triangular piece of land it was built on. What do you think, is a tent a structure? What about a ramshackle wooden hut?"

The three men chuckled and agreed that the technicality was too feeble to consider.

"It isn't a legal matter anyway," said Ellery Beaver, getting down to brass tacks. "It doesn't matter who owns the ground. It's what this Nifto goon is doing to our good name. He claims the university is letting people freeze on our doorstep while we spend billions on textual problems in the poetry of ancient Greece."

The Dean smiled ruefully. "You know, looked at in a certain way, it's true. I've often wondered why we don't give the heave-ho to half the classics department. And East Asian studies! Elementary Mongolian, my God!"

"The truth is," said the General Counsel, "we need the advice and counsel of Hamilton Dow. If the President of this institution were on hand he'd solve the problem in jigtime."

"I must say," said Ellery Beaver cautiously, "I wonder at the wisdom of the Corporation in granting the President of Harvard a sabbatical. Surely, if his job means anything at all, then the ship is without a helmsman all the time he's away."

"Foundering, you might say," agreed the Dean. "Where the hell is Ham, anyway?"

"Up the Amazon, I gather, in a dugout canoe," groaned the General Counsel, "a thousand miles from civilization. Wouldn't you know he'd put himself completely out of touch?"

"*However,*" said Ellery Beaver, leaning forward to make a significant point, "think about it! If Ham Dow were here, what would he do? He'd cave in. He'd agree to everything Nifto asked for. Pretty soon we'd be building a high-rise in the middle of Harvard Yard for all the homeless men, women, and children in the Commonwealth of Massachusetts."

"Oh, my God, you're right," said the Dean.

"Christ, I didn't think of that," said the General Counsel.

"The first thing Ham would do would be to get his friends in the Corporation all excited. You know, people like Shackleton Bowditch and Julia Chamberlain. Then who knows what the hell would happen?"

"But he's away," said the Dean. "Praise be to God for his manifold blessings. Oh, say, Ellery, why isn't your boss here? Ernest's not on sabbatical too?"

Ellery Beaver rose and stood with his back to one of the windows and arranged his face with care. His expression was half the warm smile of a kindly and compassionate man, the old friend and disciple of Ernest Henshaw, and half the grin of a wolf closing in for the kill. "Just between you and me . . ."

In gripping detail he divulged the sad story of the mental deterioration of his chief, while the others listened in fascinated horror. A burning question was uppermost at once. If Henshaw really was over the hill, who would take his place?

It was apparent to the General Counsel and the Dean of the Faculty of Arts and Sciences that Henshaw's assistant, Associate Dean Ellery Beaver, was a rising man.

◇ ◇ ◇ ◇ ◇ ◇ ◇ ◇ ◇ ◇ ◇ ◇

PART FOUR

THE LORD OF MISRULE

Nowell, nowell, nowell,
Nowell sing we loud!
God hath this day poor folk raised,
And cast adown the proud!
Carol, "Masters in This Hall"

◇ ◇ ◇ ◇ ◇ ◇ ◇ ◇ ◇ ◇ ◇ ◇

CHAPTER 24

Wassail, wassail, all over the town,
Our cup is white and our ale is brown.
The cup is made from the old oak tree,
And the ale is made in Kentucky,
So it's joy to you and a jolly wassail!
Kentucky wassail

Palmer Nifto's little plan burst full-blown on the world that evening. A bunch of Revels people were present at the beginning, after taking in a movie at the theatre on Church Street and eating a late supper together in Harvard Square.

There were six of them—Morgan and Sarah Bailey, Walt Shattuck, Arlo Field, Jeffery Peck, and Kevin Barnes. At dinner some of the cherries were still stuck in Kevin's hair.

Crowded into a booth in the Wursthaus, relaxing over their beers, they might have had a good time if Dr. Box hadn't suddenly appeared among them. Eagerly she hauled up a chair and parked it at their table, blocking the aisle. All she wanted, she said, was a glass of tomato juice and a chance to explain the true meaning of the horn dance as an ancient hunter-gatherer ritual ensuring success in the chase.

Arlo Field didn't bother to listen. He sat gazing at Sarah—stupidly, unconsciously—until he caught her husband looking at him. At once he dropped his eyes to his beer. Dr. Box talked on and on. Walt murmured a comment now and then, gently protesting, because he knew a lot more about the old rituals than did Dr. Box. Kevin gazed at the ceiling and shook his head to make

his cherries waggle, Jeffery Peck snickered, and Sarah's courtesy was sorely tested. Her baby was a lead weight inside her.

They came out of the Wursthaus to find Harvard Square jiggeting with life. People were thick on the sidewalks, crowded at the crossings. They ascended and descended the subway stairs. A fat woman in a black leather coat jerked to the secret music of her earphones, an old guy in a fur hat held up a copy of the newspaper *Spare Change*, a long-haired kid recited his poetry in front of the Harvard Coop, taxis pulled away from the sidewalk, the Peruvian band sang loudly in Spanish, and a graceful black man on Rollerblades swooped in and out among the cars on Massachusetts Avenue.

Sarah dropped a coin in front of an old man crouched in a blanket in front of the Unitarian church. He didn't pick it up. Was he asleep? Glancing back, she saw his dark hand creep out and in again.

Morgan and Sarah said good night to the others and started across the street to wait for the bus to Inman Square, but just then a large truck came out of nowhere and blocked Massachusetts Avenue. The driver leaned out the window and argued with a couple of policemen. A familiar-looking guy in dark shades was arguing too, talking a blue streak.

"Who's that?" said Sarah, looking at the man in dark glasses. "Doesn't he hang around that tent city of homeless people?"

Morgan didn't know, nor did he care. He was content to have Sarah's arm in his, to have no competition for her attention at last.

They dodged around the obstruction while people shouted at the truck from the stalled cars on Garden Street. Stuck in the teeming traffic on Massachusetts Avenue, frustrated drivers blew their horns.

The truck was heaped high, packed tight—puffy arm to puffy arm, sagging seat to flabby pillowed back—with seventeen of Palmer Nifto's drab upholstered requisitioned sofas.

CHAPTER 25

From the East the donkey came,
Stout and strong as twenty men;
Ears like wings and eyes like flame,
Striding into Bethlehem.
Heh! Sir Ass, oh heh!
"Orientis Partibus"

It was 4:00 a.m. in Harvard Square. The traffic jam had calmed down. The three-quarter moon shone bald and bright in the sky above the truck that was double-parked on Garden Street, as Palmer Nifto and the truck driver and Bob Chumley tried to manhandle the first sofa down on the pavement.

Half the citizens of Harvard Towers waited on the sidewalk. Bob's dogs frisked and barked and tangled one another in their leashes. Vergil Taylor skimmed in and out, executing phenomenal leaps on and off the curb, while his boom box thundered and crashed. A guy from the *Cambridge Chronicle*, summoned by Palmer Nifto, leaned against a light pole, yawning.

"Okay," said Palmer, "here we go. Put the first one down right here."

The driver of the truck was mystified. "But this is a major intersection. It's Harvard Square. You can't dump sofas on the street in Harvard Square."

"Why not? Come on, Bob, you take the other end." Palmer jumped down and grasped the stumpy legs of the sofa, and it came down with a thump.

"But, Jesus, Palmer," said the driver, "this is a parking place, for Christ's sake."

"Why, so it is," said Palmer. He plucked a quarter out of his pocket and popped it in the meter. "There we are. Perfectly legal. All we're doing is parking."

The guy from the *Cambridge Chronicle* guffawed and took a picture, Bob Chumley snickered, and his dogs leaped into the truck and hopped up on another sofa.

"Here, Guthrie," said Palmer, beckoning to the old man, "this one's for you. Just lie down and make yourself comfortable, okay?"

Guthrie shuffled forward and stared uneasily at the humpy shape of the sofa, which looked very strange on the edge of a broad city avenue in the middle of Harvard Square, somebody's derelict *three-cushioned high-backed buttery-soft vinyl sofa with lumbar support,* bought years ago at a sleazy furniture store in Central Square. "You mean here? This sofa right here? Listen, I want to tell you something, I ain't going to lie down on a piece of crap like that there sofa."

"Now, come on, Guthrie. It's a nice comfy sofa, and it's all yours. And, hey, looky here, I've got a blanket." Palmer nipped into the cab of the truck, hauled out an army blanket, and tucked Guthrie in like a loving mother with an infant child. "Cozy as a bug in a rug, Guthrie. Now, just make yourself comfortable and lie down and go to sleep."

Guthrie lay down cautiously, then reared up again. "Listen, I want to tell you something. The police, they ain't gonna like it."

"What's not to like?" Palmer beamed with righteousness. "I put in a quarter. We're parking here, that's all we're doing. Go to sleep now, Guthrie, there's a good boy."

Guthrie lay down again, but he kept lifting his head to watch Palmer Nifto and Bob Chumley and the bemused driver of the truck dump sofa after sofa down on the parking spaces along Garden Street.

"My God, Nifto, what's all this?" Arlo Field was on his way to the Science Center to begin dawn observations of the rising sun with the spectrohelioscope. He stopped to gaze at the row of battered sofas.

Palmer explained, while his crew of homeless men and women plopped themselves on the sofas and hauled up Palmer's blankets and settled down. Bob Chumley took charge of the meters, moving up and down the line, popping in quarters, and the truck driver backed his truck a little farther up the street to dump the last couple of sofas.

"Hey, like my meter's gonna run out," hollered Guthrie, at the other end of the row, in sofa number one.

"Right you are." Bob raced back, accompanied by his dogs, and dropped in a quarter.

Arlo started to laugh. He couldn't stop. He was still laughing when a police cruiser pulled up beside Palmer and a couple of uniformed women got out and said, "What the *hell* is going on?"

"Just a sec." Palmer guided the last sofa down from the truck into a parking place next to the old cemetery. The sofa was a baroque affair with a busted leg. It came down with a bang, and another leg broke off. The sofa tipped crazily on its remaining legs, but Palmer beckoned to Gretchen Milligan to lie down on its gritty velvet surface.

Gretchen was game. "Whoops," she said, laughing. "It's, like, rocking." The sofa settled back with a bump against the curb, and she nestled herself into the cushions.

"You see?" said Palmer to the two policewomen, dropping a quarter in Gretchen's meter. "She's paying her way.

It's all perfectly straightforward. If rich people's cars can have homes on the street, merely by paying a quarter, so can we. You want to speak to my attorney?"

The two women looked at Nifto, flabbergasted. Their mouths were open, but nothing came out. Then the shorter one had a flash of genius. "Wheeled vehicles," she said firmly. "These parking spaces are exclusively for the use of wheeled vehicles. Get these sofas out of here. Come on, Palmer, get 'em out. Right now. You hear what I said? Move them out of here right now."

"Okay, Palmer," said the truck driver wearily, "we better load 'em up again. Oh, God, I'm tired."

"Hey, Palmer," said Arlo, "wait a minute. Come here, listen, I've got an idea."

Palmer listened, and then he turned away from Arlo and grinned at the two women in uniform. "Okay, okay," he said, "out they go again. Come on, Bob, let's load 'em up."

"But, shit, Palmer," said Bob, who was tired of humping sofas, "like we just—"

"I know." Palmer helped Gretchen heave herself out of the broken sofa. "But we've got to be law-abiding, don't we, Bob?"

"Here," said Arlo cheerfully. "I'll help."

Bulging enormously, Gretchen stood on the sidewalk and watched as the driver of the truck and Bob Chumley and Palmer Nifto and Arlo Field helped the other occupants out of the sofas and hoisted all seventeen bulky pieces of furniture back onto the truck, piling them on top of one another, right side up and upside down.

The sofa caper was over, and the sleepy citizens of Harvard Towers began shuffling back to their tent city. But Gretchen Milligan looked back regretfully. "It was so comfortable," she said. "I mean, that sofa was really comfortable."

"God," said one of the policewomen to her partner as they drove away, "what will they think of next?"

. . . gladly, good lord, would I game here and sleep,
But I have a quest and a promise to keep.
                    "Sir Gawain and the Green Knight"

It was true that Homer had washed his hands of the two Revels tragedies, the deaths of Henry Shady and Tom Cobb, leaving both matters up to the investigative branches of the Harvard and Cambridge Police Departments. But as time went on, Homer's fatal curiosity was getting the better of him.

There had been nothing in the papers about the real cause of Cobb's death, and nothing on the local television news, only the report that he had swallowed a toxic substance. But the rumor that he had been poisoned was everywhere, and Homer wanted to get to the bottom of it.

He had long since forgotten his wife's idiotic concern over the first Revels death, the accident that had killed Henry Shady—her wild story about some crazy goose and the problem of timing and some other dumb thing— what was it? No matter. It didn't make sense. His wife, Mary, was a superb human being, a wonderful companion, a warm and responsive lover, a magnificent teacher and a fine writer, but she didn't know beans about the investigation of criminal activity.

Was that why she'd been a little testy lately? Probably. Mary was just a little jealous of his long-standing expertise, all that know-how he had picked up so long ago as a lieutenant detective for Middlesex County. Jealousy, God! It was a pain in the neck.

Unfortunately, Homer's vast experience couldn't help

him now. By rights he should have been able to go straight to the Cambridge Police Department to find out more about the toxic substance that had killed Tom Cobb, but he couldn't. His personal and official relation with the department was poor. *Excessive interference on the part of an unaccredited person*—that was the way they had put it.

Well, of course they were right. While poking into certain matters in the recent past, Homer had found it necessary to flash his long-outdated identification card as a Middlesex County lieutenant detective. The Cambridge investigating officer had seen through him, and he had barely escaped arrest. So in this matter he would have to be completely on his own.

Was the rumor true, that Cobb had been poisoned? How could he find out?

On the afternoon after Palmer Nifto's sofa caper in Harvard Square, Homer made his way to Cambridge Hospital. It was only a few blocks east of Memorial Hall, on Cambridge Street.

Approaching the front entrance, he felt like the heroic protagonist of one of Dr. Box's vision quests. In order to behold the vision or find the Grail or achieve whatever fabulous goal lay at the end of the quest, he would first have to overcome a set of impossible obstacles.

The hospital receptionist was the first enchanted obstacle. She was a mountain of glass.

Homer's magic talisman was his famous charm. Leaning over the counter, he showed all his teeth and complimented her on her navy-blue suit.

The magic failed. The receptionist was a severe young woman who at once detected the sexist nature of this ploy. "Get to the point," she said sharply, with a look like a splinter from the glass mountain.

"Can you tell me how to find the pathologist's office?" said Homer humbly.

"Third floor," barked the receptionist. Whirling around in her chair, she began rattling the keyboard of her computer at high speed.

"Thank you," breathed Homer. Rambling down the hall, he found the elevator. The first obstacle had been overcome, if somewhat feebly. The second would be a seven-headed mastiff with a thousand bloodstained teeth.

The door labeled PATHOLOGY was wide open. Homer walked in and found a medical technician in a white coat riffling through a file drawer. She turned her head in Homer's direction and raised her eyebrows. With her long golden hair and pink cheeks she didn't look like a mastiff at all, but Homer was wary.

"I'd like to see the report of the toxicologist on the death of Thomas Cobb," said Homer, trying to sound businesslike and bored, as though the matter were strictly ho-hum.

"Right you are," said the technician. Briskly she yanked out another file drawer and extracted a folder. But instead of handing it over, she looked at Homer suspiciously. "May I ask your authority for requesting this information?"

Seven doggy heads had sprouted from her shoulders. *Oh Christ,* thought Homer. Whisking out his bag of amulets, he produced his old identity card. True, its magic had been discredited by the Cambridge Police Department, but since then he had encased it in plastic. It looked shiny and new.

Damn the woman, she was holding it under a lamp and examining it closely, while clutching the folder to her breast. When she looked up at him gravely, blood dripped from her seven cavernous jaws. "This card is fifteen years out of date. May I ask if you are still employed by the District Attorney of Middlesex County?"

Little white lies came easily to Homer's lips, but outright falsehoods did not, especially one that could be exposed by a simple phone call. "Well, no, but I've had considerable experience since then in investigative matters. You might have heard of the explosion in Memorial Hall, for example, or the ax attack in Amherst? No? What about the body in Gowing's Swamp? You mean to tell me you never heard of that?" Homer racked his brain for more of his blundering triumphs, while the medical technician looked at him with deep suspicion.

Then victory fell into his hands. It was one of those sudden miracles that are apt to happen in vision quests upon the arrival of angelic visitants.

In this case the angels were a couple of cadavers. One arrived from the east, the other from the west. Their gurneys nearly collided in the corridor. The medics accompanying them at once began arguing about which dead body was to be signed in first. In the confusion the golden-haired guardian of the Pathology office left her post and joined the fracas in the hall.

Left to himself, Homer reached for the autopsy report on the body of Thomas Cobb. Swiftly he leafed through it, and at once found what he was looking for.

The gums of the deceased, explained the toxicologist, showed a significant blue line. His stomach contained a gummy mixture of chocolate, corn syrup, sugar, soybean oil, milk, cocoa powder, malt, lactose, salt, egg white, peanut butter, and a substantial quantity of arsenate of lead.

Homer had found his Holy Grail.

Sarah Bailey was expecting half a dozen of her colleagues for a committee meeting. The costume designer, the music director, the stage manager, the lighting designer, and the sound engineer, they were all coming. They would need chairs to sit on. She raced around the apartment on Maple Avenue, rearranging furniture. She tidied up the sink, swabbed the counter, picked up the books and papers from the floor, swept up the dead leaves under a dying houseplant, and made the bed. Then she dumped the contents of the wastebasket into a plastic bag, and whirled the bag to twist and knot the top. At once she untwisted it again to take a look at the trash.

What were those little brown papers doing in there? They looked like candy wrappers. They *were* candy wrappers. *Tastychox,* the wrappers said. It was that rich, delicious kind of chocolate that Tom Cobb had liked so well.

That was odd. Sarah didn't buy candy and neither did Morgan. Candy, as far as they were concerned, was deadly poison.

CHAPTER 27

Brightest and best of the sons of the morning!
Dawn on our darkness and lend us thine aid . . .
                                    Appalachian folk hymn

T he sun hung sluggishly at the bottom of the analemma. It seemed stuck, as though it would never climb to the pinnacle of June.

On the eighth floor of the Science Center, Arlo checked on his camera, which was still firmly anchored to the floor with duct tape.

He looked at his watch. Did he have time to look for a Christmas present for his mother? She had called yesterday and made it plain that he was not to forget. *Now, dear, don't spend too much money on my present. Oh, I've bought you such a lovely gift!*

The trouble was, he didn't have the faintest idea where to start. His mother was a loving and sentimental widow, and Arlo, she said, was her only chick and child. So far, his close acquaintance with the opposite sex had been only with his mother, Cindy the hockey player, and Totty the believer in astral energy. It didn't give him much faith in women. He looked at the pretty girls in his classes, he enjoyed his friendship with Chickie Pickett, and he felt a hunger for sexual intimacy with some woman or other, some time, somehow. He imagined getting married and having children, but—God!—was there a sensible person out there anywhere, somebody to love and admire at the same time?

Now, dear, don't spend too much money on my present!

One of the mirrors that bounced the sun's image onto

the observation table flickered, and Arlo glanced up. A face looked back at him for an instant. Oh, well, hell, it was Sarah Bailey. His psyche or aura or innermost spiritual being was judging him, telling him he was falling in love again. What a dumb idea.

Then Arlo forgot his lugubrious analysis of the women in his life as Harley Finch came in and began barging around the room, looking for a book. "Where the hell did I put it?"

"Hey, watch it, Harley, you almost bumped into my camera."

"Oh, sorry."

Harley was a big round-shouldered guy with thinning light hair and pop eyes. There were a number of large pale moles on his fat arms. Arlo often thought of him as an emission spectrum with a single bright line, his gift for abstract mathematics. Harley was a theoretician. He had no skill with mechanical things, he knew nothing about art or literature or music or history or the state of world affairs, and yet, oddly enough, he had a firm grasp on departmental politics.

It occurred to Arlo to ask him about the rumor that somebody was about to be fired. "Any more news about shrinkage in the department?"

Harley found his book and headed for the door. He looked embarrassed. "I don't know. They say there'll be an announcement soon."

He did know, but he wasn't telling. Arlo guessed the worst.

Oh, God, never mind. He had a class to prepare for, a whole lecture hall full of kids taking Astronomy 1. It was a course for non–science majors, some of whom were so ignorant they didn't know which was farther away, the sun or the moon. Arlo spent much of his time explaining the basic principles of physics.

Today it was Newton's third law, *To every action there is an equal and opposite reaction.* Arlo snatched up his lecture notes and ran down seven flights to consult with the clever engineers in the Prep Room, who spent their time constructing gadgets for the teaching of any kind of scientific principle. They built contraptions to demonstrate simple things like inclined planes, or complex things like the systems of mirrors and lenses in a telescope.

Today they were providing him with a really funny

demonstration, a full-size vehicle that would whiz across the lecture hall, propelled by CO_2 cartridges.

"Is it ready?" said Arlo.

"You bet." The mechanical engineer wheeled it forward, grinning with pride. "Here she is, the Isaac Newton Whizbang."

"That's great," said Arlo. "Oh, say, that reminds me." He looked around the Prep Room at the rows of shelves. "Have you guys got any wheels?"

CHAPTER 28

. . . And a box of my pills, take one tonight and two
in the morning, and swallow the box at dinner time.
If the box don't cure you, the lid will.
Traditional British Mummers' Play

"Homer? This is Sarah. Now, listen, Homer, dear."

Homer was on his way out the door with a battery charger. His car was dead, and his poor wife was trying to get her own car up the steep icy driveway. Through the window he could see her attack the hill again. No, goddamnit, she was running out of steam halfway up and backing down again. He snarled into the phone, "Well, go ahead, I'm listening."

"It's Buck, he's come down with flu."

"Buck? Who's Buck?" *Gun it, Mary, gun it.*

"Buck Zemowski, you remember Buck. He plays Father Christmas."

"Oh, right." *Good, good, that's good! You're going to make it! Oh, no—no—oh, damn.*

"He's sick, so, please, Homer, I want you to take over his part."

"Who, me? Not on your life." *Come on, girl, start way back in the bushes this time.*

Sarah went on talking, urging, persuading. Homer stared out the window. He was only barely listening. *Why the hell did they live in this crazy place? Winter on the river was absolutely impossible.*

In the end Sarah talked him into it. Mary's fourth attempt to mount the hill was successful, and Homer was so relieved, he said, "Well, okay, Sarah, anything you say."

Of course he was sorry almost immediately, but Sarah thanked him so affectionately and hung up so quickly, there was no opportunity to back out.

Later on, after his last pre-Christmas class, Homer reported for duty in the great hall to be fitted with the red robe belonging to Father Christmas.

"Hey, that's great," said Joan Hill. "Buck needed a pillow to make him fat enough, but you don't need a pillow at all. Isn't that marvelous!"

"Thanks a lot," growled Homer.

Sarah too was delighted with Homer in his new persona. She handed him a script. "See, Homer, you stand around while Saint George is killed and then you encourage the Doctor to bring him back to life. It's a really funny scene. Come on, they're waiting for you."

Homer did his best. It was another opportunity to show off. "Pray, Doctor," he roared, "what diseases can you cure?"

"All sorts of diseases," began the Doctor, opening his black bag, "whatever you pleases. The itch, the stitch"—reaching into the bag, he took out a bicycle pump—"the palsy and the gout, raging pain both inside and out!"

It was Homer's turn, but he had forgotten his line. It occurred to him to inquire whether Saint George had recently been exposed to arsenate of lead, but, no, that wasn't right. Homer looked down at Arlo Field and invented a line of his own. "Well, Doctor, he's a long time coming back to life. The Harvard Community Health Plan is going to hear about this."

Everybody laughed, and then it was the turn of the Fool, a computer programmer from Lexington—

Stand aside; I'll fetch him back to life,
If this man's not dead, but in a trance,
We'll raise him up and have a dance!

Bending tenderly over Saint George, he laid a sprig of holly on his breast. At once Arlo raised his head, as if awakening from a deep sleep.

"No, no, Saint George," urged Jeffery Peck, "wait a little longer. We need more suspense."

Obediently Arlo dropped his head and closed his eyes. Then slowly he lifted his head again, got to his feet, and sang his song of resurrection—

Good morning, gentlemen,
a-sleeping I have been.
I've had such a sleep as the like was never seen.

Arlo's voice was creaky and uneven, but Sarah smiled at him encouragingly, and then Walt came forward to sing "The Lord of the Dance." When the performances began, all the people in the audience would join hands and dance out into the corridor—

Dance, then, wherever you may be,
I am the Lord of the Dance, said he,
And I'll lead you all, wherever you may be,
And I'll lead you all in the Dance, said he.

Mary picked up her coat and started after Homer. It was time to go home. But as she left Sanders, she witnessed a classic little melodrama in the back of the hall.

Sarah Bailey and Jeff Peck were sitting close together in whispered conference. Something struck them funny.

They laughed, and Jeff put his arm around Sarah and squeezed her shoulder. Across the hall Mary could see Morgan Bailey staring at them, his face expressionless.

At once her amateur psychological analysis reasserted itself. She remembered how miserable it had made her to see Homer goggling at that bewitching student of his— what was her name? Dora Somebody—Dora of the shining brown eyes and the long black hair. Homer, the idiot, had gaped at her and followed her around like a pet dog. It had never occurred to him, the fathead, to wonder what his wife was thinking. What dolts men were!

Mary shrugged, and pushed through the swinging door as the Abbotts Bromley horn dancers came onstage with heavy rhythmic tread. She felt sorry for Morgan, but it wasn't her problem. The poor guy was making his own hell.

Across the floor of Sanders Theatre, on the other side of the mezzanine among the seats in the third row, the hell was real. *Oh, God, look at his hand! He's groping under her shirt! Why doesn't she stop him? Oh, God, Sarah! Sarah, my God!*

With a wrench, Morgan looked away from Jeff and Sarah and tried to focus his attention on the horn dancers. They had mesmerized him in the past, with their ancient figures, their solemn twirling and turning. It was a salute to wildness, a reverence for the hunted beast. Morgan had the same reverence for his own wild geese, the same identification with that other empire populating the earth—the deer in the forest, the fish in the sea, the birds in the air.

But it didn't help Morgan's wretchedness that the next thing on the rehearsal schedule was "The Cherry Tree Carol." There they were, coming on stage, Joseph and Mary and the cherry tree. The guitar struck up its plangent

chords, Kevin Barnes held up his arms like branches, and
Walt began to sing. The young girl who played the part of
Mary made beseeching gestures to Joseph, begging him to
pick her some cherries because she was with child, and
Joseph stamped his feet in rage—

>*"Let the father of the baby*
>*Gather cherries for thee!"*

Was it on purpose? Had Sarah put it on the program on
purpose for Morgan to see?

Outdoors, Mary Kelly pulled her scarf up around her face
and Homer clamped on a pair of earmuffs. The weather
was raw, and the damp east wind penetrated to the bone.
They made their way through the ramshackle village of
Harvard Towers, and Mary wondered how its citizens
were enduring the cold. "Look, Homer, some of them are
gone."

Homer wasn't surprised to see fewer tents. Making a
quick survey, he counted only thirty. The population had
begun to decline. "Well, no wonder they're leaving, with
weather like this."

"How do the rest of them stand it?" Hurrying away
with Homer into the Yard, Mary vowed to come back tomorrow with a bagful of coats and blankets.

It was true that the enthusiasm of the homeless citizens
of Harvard Towers was waning. They were tired of freezing, tired of Portapotties, tired of being bossed around by
Palmer Nifto, tired of the mess of sleeping bags and bundles of clothing and electric heaters and crazy rigged-up
lamps in their tents, tired of being dirty, tired of having
their sad gray faces photographed for television, tired of

being chivied around by scandalized firefighters and policemen, tired of cold coffee, tired of kind people who
wanted to help but didn't have a clue what their lives were
really like.

But there were fewer departures than Homer had
guessed. The territory of Harvard Towers had stretched to
include the the west porch of Memorial Hall. A dozen
wadded shapes crouched there out of the wind.

A counselor from Bright Day House walked past them,
looking at their faces, inquiring for Gretchen Milligan. The
pregnant teenager was missing again. Had anyone seen
her? They all shook their heads.

"Foolish girl," said the counselor. "She shouldn't be out
in the cold. Not at a time like this!"

Jeffery Peck found three things in his mailbox when he
got home to his apartment on Shepard Street—an overdue
notice from the Cambridge Electric Light Company, a
wistful postcard from his sister wanting to know if he was
coming home for Christmas, and a letter. The bill and the
postcard had been delivered by the U.S. Postal Service, but
the letter had not been stamped. Someone had delivered it
by hand.

In the dim light of the entry Jeff tore open the envelope
and read the letter. With a whoop of delight he read it
again.

It was from Sarah Bailey.

CHAPTER 29

His the doom, ours the mirth . . .
Carol, "Personent Hodie"

"Wheeled vehicles only," the policewoman had said, groping for a reason to eliminate seventeen sofas from the parking spaces on Garden Street.

"No problem," said Arlo Field to Palmer Nifto. "Wheeled vehicles it shall be."

They spent the entire night of December twenty-first at the Furniture Bank, attaching wheels to a dozen of the sofas.

It was easy enough for Arlo to stay awake. As a graduate student he had spent many a long night in the open dome of the observatory at Sacramento Peak making long exposures of the spectra of faint stars.

Palmer too seemed tireless. They worked companionably side by side, drilling holes in the legs of the sofas, attaching the wheels with miscellaneous sizes of threaded bolts.

"They don't have to, like, work," explained Palmer, turning off his electric drill.

"I know," said Arlo. "It's just sort of a gag." He untangled a set of Prep Room bicycle wheels and mounted them with Palmer's help on a battered love seat. Standing up, they beamed at the result. The love seat reared up on its four wheels, ready to coast down Massachusetts Avenue.

"All it needs is a steering wheel," said Arlo. "Did you call the *Chronicle*?"

"Oh, you bet. They'll be there. TV too. First thing this morning, I said. You got to have your action early if you want to get on the evening news."

"You sure know a lot of stuff about the real world." Arlo smiled to himself, thinking of the immense stretches of space beyond the galaxy about which he knew a great deal more than Palmer Nifto. Which was the real world?

"Another thing," said Palmer. "We've got to get this stuff on the street early. If they arrest you on Friday afternoon, you spend the whole weekend in jail."

It was a public-relations bonanza. Palmer Nifto had his sofas lined up neatly on Garden Street by six o'clock in the morning, with a dozen people from Harvard Towers to occupy them. Bob Chumley was there, along with Guthrie Jones, Vergil Taylor, and old man Maggody. There they were, twelve homeless people bedded down on twelve sofas in twelve parking places in Harvard Square, just as they had been before—but now all the broken-down ratty-looking sofas were equipped with wheels—baby-carriage wheels, little-red-wagon wheels, lawn-mower wheels, and bicycle wheels. One sported automobile tires scrounged by Palmer Nifto from a wrecked-car lot.

Arlo Field had phoned Mary and Homer Kelly. They

drove in from Concord and made themselves useful. Mary moved up and down the sidewalk, dropping quarters into parking meters. Homer felt righteous, rebellious, and swaggering. He hadn't done anything so politically audacious since the Vietnam War. "We'll probably be arrested," he said, grinning at Arlo Field.

"That's okay," said Arlo from the depths of his new knowledge. "It's early. Good time for it."

All the people passing through Harvard Square on their way to work got the joke about the wheels on the sofas. Palmer had seen to that. Last week the words of the police sergeant had been emblazoned in all the local papers, and even in the *Boston Globe*—WHEELED VEHICLES ONLY, DEMANDS POLICEWOMAN; HOMELESS SOFAS TICKETED.

They got the joke and laughed and dropped money in the tin cans Palmer set out on the sidewalk.

The Cambridge police sergeant laughed too, when she came charging up in her cruiser. She couldn't help it, the sofas looked so funny. She tried to control herself, but she kept bursting out again in whoop after whoop. "You're under arrest," she gasped at last, wiping her eyes and grinning. "Palmer Nifto, I am placing you under arrest."

"Whatever for?" said Palmer innocently, spreading out his hands. He pulled Homer Kelly forward. "May I introduce my attorney?"

"My God, Nifto, I'm not your attorney," whispered Homer.

"Mr. Kelly will insist upon a written certificate of arrest, naming the law we have violated. Right, Mr. Kelly?"

"Oh, sure, sure," mumbled Homer, looking at the woman officer in embarrassment, "you've got to have a warrant to arrest anybody."

But she was whipping a pad of forms out of her pocket.

"Disturbing the peace, that's one count. I'll think of some more in a minute."

"Disturbing the peace? I'm not disturbing the peace." Palmer turned to the row of sofas and spoke up loudly to the twelve occupants, who were sitting up and staring at the police sergeant. "We're simply sleeping, peacefully sleeping, that's all we're doing." At once they flopped back down.

"You made me laugh, that's how you disturbed the peace." The police officer giggled. "I probably woke up a bunch of people living around here."

"Where?" Wide-eyed, Palmer gestured at the tombstones behind the iron fence. "In the cemetery?"

It was the funniest thing to appear on the local television news in years. Of course Palmer had to load up his sofas again, and take them back to the Furniture Bank, but he had made his point. The homeless people of Cambridge were once more the center of attention.

And that afternoon their fame attracted the defectors back. By four o'clock there were eighty-one campers at Harvard Towers. The good women of the Congregational church had to make a second vat of split-pea soup, and rush over to Sage's to get more eggs for the cornbread. The loyal kids from Phillips Brooks House turned out batch after batch of cookies.

"Oh, God, I keep burning them," said Millie, the idealistic freshman, yanking another tin out of the oven and slapping it down on the counter.

"Just scrape off the black," said Brad, the idealistic sophomore.

That evening, back home in Concord, Homer and Mary turned on the news to see if Palmer Nifto had succeeded in attracting national publicity. Oh, yes, he had. There he was, and there were the sofas with their wheels, and there was the anchorwoman announcing that in Cambridge, Massachusetts, where these homeless people were living in tents out-of-doors, the temperature was about to plummet to ten degrees below zero.

The next piece of news was also of flabbergasting interest.

"General Confection," said the anchorwoman, "the manufacturer of many popular brands of candies and candy bars, is rushing to take off grocers' shelves the product believed to have caused the death of Thomas Cobb of Cambridge, Massachusetts. Arsenate of lead was found in Cobb's stomach, which otherwise contained only the ingredients of a candy bar called Tastychox. Some malicious person is thought to have injected the bar with this highly toxic substance. No other illnesses connected with Tastychox have been reported, but shoppers are warned to avoid it."

"A candy bar!" said Homer. "Of course, I should have guessed. All that chocolate and cocoa powder and so on. Naturally, it was a candy bar." He looked at his wife in triumph. "So it was murder, all right, just as I thought. Somebody injected Tom's candy bar with arsenate of lead. What the hell for? What did anybody have against him? Mary, dear, for Christ's sake, what's the matter? You're white as a sheet."

"Homer, oh, Homer." Mary jumped to her feet, but she was too weak to stand up. Sinking back in her chair, she tried to explain it. She could only tell it in short bursts, how Tom had offered her his candy bar, how he had taken it out of his pocket and held it out to her only an hour or two before he fell writhing to the floor of the stage in Sanders Theatre. If she had accepted it, if she had not already used up her appetite on a liverwurst sandwich and a couple of sugary doughnuts, *she* was the one

who would have died in anguish on the operating table. "Oh, Homer."

Homer said nothing, he merely swept her up and held her in his arms.

Gretchen Milligan had still not come back to Bright Day. Her counselor went out in the cold to look for her at Harvard Towers and in the shelters at University Lutheran and Central Square, but no one knew where Gretchen was.

The counselor was darkly pessimistic. "Don't blame me," she said to the other social workers at Bright Day when she got back and climbed the steep steps to the front door and warmed her cold fingers around a mug of hot coffee. "Don't blame me if we have a dead mother and a stillborn child on our hands. What else can I do?"

CHAPTER 30

> *O then bespoke Joseph,*
> *With answer most unkind,*
> *"Let him pluck thee a cherry*
> *That brought thee now with child."*
> "The Cherry Tree Carol"

A rlo Field came running back to the astronomy lab in the middle of the hilarious encounter between the Cambridge Police Department and Palmer Nifto. Something more important was on Arlo's mind.

It was Friday, December twenty-second, the shortest day of the year. He had an appointment with his camera. He wanted to be on hand at eight-thirty in the morning to make sure it took its last picture of the sun, the image that would appear on the film at the very lowest point of the curve of the analemma. Then he would remove the filter and set the timer to take a picture later on in normal light, to give foreground to the forty-four bright suns in the dark sky—a view of the tower of Memorial Hall in the normal sunshine of afternoon. Thank God, it was a clear day.

Arlo was early enough in the astronomy lab to have time on his hands. He ambled around the room staring at the floor, thinking about sofas, shutter speeds, solar flares, and Sarah Bailey. It wasn't until he had looked at the marks on the floor three times that he at last really saw them.

The legs of the tripod had been moved. They were taped to the floor, but they were not on the marks.

Alarmed, enraged, he dropped to his knees, tore off the tape, moved the camera back, and shifted it by small de-

grees until the little scope showed the northeastern gee-
gaw on the top of the Mem Hall tower. Then he taped the
tripod down again.

Who the hell would do a thing like that? God, it couldn't
have been Chickie Pickett? Chickie was pretty wild, but
she really cared about the analemma project. It couldn't
have been Chickie.

A lot of other students hung around the lab, and some
of them were pretty nutty.

Arlo stood up and stared thoughtfully at the camera. *Let
us now consider Harley Finch.* Harley had nearly knocked the
camera down once already, because he was clumsy. But
this dirty trick wasn't mere clumsiness. Someone had used
great care in pulling off the old tape and fastening the legs
down in the wrong places. Harley was the only person
with a reason for discrediting the work of Arlo Field. He'd
be ensuring his own academic survival.

Grimly Arlo looked at his watch. There was still half an
hour to kill before the last exposure of the sun at eight-
thirty. Bored, he went out on the terrace and leaned
against the railing, looking out over the city of Cambridge
and Harvard University. Directly below him was Palmer
Nifto's tent city of homeless people. Some of them were
straggling back from the sofa caper in Harvard Square.
Yes, there was Nifto, walking briskly in the direction of his
command center with a cameraman in tow.

Then Arlo gripped the railing and leaned over a little
farther to stare at Sarah and Morgan Bailey. They were
walking quickly along Kirkland Street, approaching the
north door of Memorial Hall.

Arlo ran into the lab for a pair of high-powered field
glasses, then ran back to the railing and aimed them at
Sarah.

As usual she was rosy and broad and beautiful, with that mop of tangled hair into which Arlo longed to plunge his fingers. But her eyes were cast down. Why did she look that way? If it weren't absurd to think it of Sarah Bailey, he would say she was frightened.

He shifted the glasses to her husband. Morgan's eyes were bright, but his face was pale with a more-than-winter paleness. In the last week Arlo had made an effort to befriend Morgan Bailey, and for a while it had worked. Morgan had his birds and Arlo his sun and stars, and each had tried to take an interest in the other's profession. But lately Morgan had seemed too absorbed in some silent business of his own to exchange small talk with Arlo Field.

And anyway—Arlo had to admit it to himself—his only reason for getting to know Morgan had been to get closer to his wife. Quickly, before she disappeared inside Mem Hall, Arlo shifted the glasses back to Sarah's face. At once it jumped up at him, and Arlo's heart jumped with it. With a wry grin, he recognized the fatal symptoms. Goddamnit, he was in love again.

Greedily he stared at Sarah as she began climbing the steps with Morgan. Then, to his dismay, she turned her head and glanced upward. She was looking straight at him through the lenses of the glasses. And, oh, God, so was Morgan. And Morgan's pale face was red with anger. His lips were moving, he was saying something, something furious, but there was no giant ear trumpet to amplify the sound, as the field glasses had magnified the sight.

At once Arlo let the glasses drop around his neck. Now Sarah and Morgan were only toy figures opening a faraway door and disappearing inside.

Trembling, Arlo went back into the lab, so agitated that he forgot to lock the glass door. He couldn't get Sarah's glance of recognition out of his mind. Had there been a look of appeal on her face? Or was his imagination working overtime?

With an effort he put her out of his mind, because it was almost eight-thirty, time for the last exposure of his camera to the sun. Would the shutter open on schedule, or had the digital alarm been monkeyed with too? If so, he'd have to depress the button by hand.

He went to the camera and watched the green numbers on the clock change from 8:25 to 8:30. *Good*—there it was, the soft buzzing click. The last solar image had been recorded. With his tongue between his teeth Arlo delicately removed the filter, changed the exposure setting, and set the timer for three o'clock. Tonight he'd try to get back here and take a look at his year's work.

The phone rang. It was his mother, calling from Pittsfield. "Arlo dear, is everything all right?"

"Of course everything's all right."

"Dear, I know you said you can only come for Christmas Day, but I'm *so* hoping you can stay a little longer?"

Arlo grimaced at his mother's pathetic tone. "But, Mom, I told you, there are Revels performances the day before Christmas and the day after. I have to be here."

"I see. Oh, Arlo, dear, I'm *so* disappointed."

Arlo relented. "Tell you what, I'll come for the next weekend, the whole long weekend."

"Oh, thank you, dear! And remember, you're not to worry about a Christmas present for me. Just any little thing will do."

Arlo said goodbye and tore out of the office, leaving the door unlocked as usual.

So the next person to step off the elevator had no trouble getting in.

Morgan entered the astronomy lab with an excuse on his lips, but to his relief the place was empty. His heart was beating rapidly, he was rigid with furious purpose.

But he was too early. Tensely he walked around Arlo's office, looking at things he didn't understand. His terrors had expanded, they were sending out fingers in all directions. Arlo Field! Just now Arlo had been staring at Sarah through some kind of powerful field glasses, he had been spying on her. Morgan's fears multiplied. Jeffery Peck was after her, anyone could see that, and so was Arlo Field, and so were all the rest. They were all after Sarah!

Jeff entered the Science Center at quarter to three precisely, and looked at Sarah's letter to be sure he was doing the right thing—*Darling, meet me at three o'clock—tomorrow in the astronomy lab.* It was a crazy place for a meeting, but what the hell did it matter? At three o'clock he would be wherever Sarah Bailey wanted him to be, down in a coal mine or up in a balloon.

The elevator took him to the eighth floor, and at once he recognized the door to the astronomy lab. It was wide open. Eagerly Jeffery went in, calling, "Sarah?"

The office was empty, but the door to the terrace was open.

"Sarah, darling," called Jeffery.

There was no answer, only an odd sort of hissing sound.

"Sarah?" he called again, and hurried outside.

But it wasn't Sarah who was waiting for him on the terrace.

The scuffle was short. Jeffery was too surprised to react. As he went over the railing he said nothing at all, but the letter in his hand left his galvanized fingers and flew away.

He fell eight floors, and landed with a thud and a crash of splintering glass on the roof of the Greenhouse cafeteria.

At once Morgan stepped back from the railing, ran into the lab and out into the hall and catapulted down three flights of stairs. On the fifth floor he quieted his thumping heart and waited for the elevator. On the ground floor he joined the thick flood of students going in and out of class. A rumor was spreading—"Hey, some guy fell"—and kids were running in the direction of the cafeteria. Morgan ignored them and walked out of the building.

In the meantime, the letter that had brought Jeffery to the eighth floor floated down, drifting this way and that, sailing high over the descending terraces of the Science Center. A strong breeze picked it up, the little white shape fluttering like a dove, and whisked it above the encampment on the overpass. Then it was blown westward, beyond the snarling traffic at the intersection of Cambridge Street and Massachusetts Avenue, to soar over the trees on Cambridge Common. There the wind gave out, and the letter floated down from branch to branch, tipping this way and that, until at last it skimmed sideways in the direction of the Civil War Memorial and came to rest in front of a dark shape sitting on the ground.

Here the frigid wind might have picked it up again and sent it scuttling across the yellowed grass, but a hand reached out—slowly, very slowly—and clutched it and did not let it go.

CHAPTER 31

This ae nighte, this ae nighte,
Everie nighte and alle,
Fire and slete and candle-lighte,
And Christe receive thy saule. . . .
                              "Lyke Wake Dirge"

O utside the cafeteria the medics from the police ambulance bowed over the body of Jeffery Peck, while Officer Plover shouted at the rubbernecking students to move back out of the way. Inside the cafeteria the manager looked at the mess of broken glass, the abandoned cups of coffee, the smashed crockery, the fallen chairs. A couple of kids had been cut by flying splinters and taken to the infirmary. Confused, in a state of shock, he walked across the floor, crunching jagged pieces of glass under his feet, and stared out at the crumpled body of Jeffery Peck.

"Christ, why didn't he jump off the top floor of William James?" he said to the checkout girl. "Tallest building around. Nice clean drop. Then we wouldn't have to sweep up all this mess. Some people are so thoughtless." It was a joke.

The news about the guy who had plummeted to his death from one of the terraces above the cafeteria courtyard flew around the Science Center, but it did not immediately make its way across the overpass to Memorial Hall. Jeff Peck was sorely missed in Sanders Theatre—the first performance would be starting shortly, so where in hell was he?—but nobody knew he was dead.

Morgan Bailey knew, but he said nothing. In the great

hall he dressed for the performance and polished the pair of clogs he had inherited from Tom Cobb.

"Hey, Sarah," said Bill Foose, "if Jeff doesn't show up, we'll be short one Morris dancer again."

"But where can he be?" said Sarah. "He wouldn't abandon us on the night of the first performance. I called him at home, but he wasn't there. Something must be the matter." Sarah's heart misgave her. Once again the overheated boiler was about to burst. The smell of the scalding steam was like a hot mist filling Memorial Hall. In her head the words went around and around: *Arsenate of lead was found in Cobb's stomach, which otherwise contained only the ingredients of a candy bar called Tastychox.*

Sarah knew nothing about the arsenate of lead Morgan kept in the trunk of the Range Rover. But she had found three Tastychox candy wrappers in the wastebasket. Morgan didn't eat candy, so why had he bought them? Why, why? The question terrified her. *And, oh, God, it was the Range Rover that had run down Henry Shady.*

"Kevin Barnes is here somewhere," said Bill Foose. "He's not as good as Jeff, but he'd be okay."

"What?" said Sarah. "Oh, right. Quickly, see if he can do it."

Fortunately, Kevin was willing. The Morris dancers loyally spent half an hour teaching him what to do. Even as he practiced the two dances and mastered the order of events, people began to crowd into the corridor, their coats frosted with snow.

The clarity of the morning sky had given way to clouds as dusk fell, and the first flakes began falling around six o'clock. In the extreme cold they were perfect crystals. By the time the twelve hundred people holding tickets to the first performance of the Christmas Revels found their seats in Sanders Theatre, the snow was coming down hard.

For a performance without a codirector and with one of the Morris dancers hauled in at the last minute, it went fairly well. Sarah was relieved, although she sensed that the attention of the audience was distracted by the storm. While Walt led them all in singing carols, and the Morris men clashed their sticks, and the children enacted "Three Billy Goats Gruff," and Joseph stamped his feet in jealous rage, all the people in the long rows of benches were wondering if their cars would start and whether the streets of Cambridge would be plowed.

But during the intermission they joined the endless chain in the memorial corridor and forgot the blizzard. Clasping hands, they danced around and around, spiraling into the center, squeezing together in the middle, shrieking with joy and spiraling out again—dignifed members of the Harvard Corporation, executives from BayBank, mothers and fathers with toddlers and teenagers, grandmothers and grandchildren.

The magic lasted through the second act, as the mummers performed the ancient roles whose sources were lost to history. Miss Funny—the man-woman with her mustache and parasol—the comic Fool, the Hobby Horse, and Little Johnny Jack with his family on his back—they were ritual figures remembered from last year and the year before. The costumes were like illuminations in a book of hours, the men and women of the chorus in long gowns and tunics of scarlet and pink and orange, cobalt blue and apple green. And then there was the haunting darkness of the horn dance, with the dancers moving in intricate patterns, holding their great antlers over their heads. And at last it was time for Saint George and his witty encounter with the dragon, and then the strangeness of his slaughter, and his revival at the hands of the funny Doctor and the

Fool. It was all familiar, wonderfully familiar. It was something people wanted to see again every year, blizzard or no blizzard.

But when the second act was over and the performers bowed at the front of the stage—the Fool and Miss Funny and the Morris dancers and Saint George and the children and all the members of the chorus—everyone in the audience came back to the real world and remembered what was going on outside.

This year the season of the solstice was winter at its worst. As they funneled out of Sanders Theatre there was an urgency in the way they hauled on their coats and hoisted sleepy children to their shoulders and moved north and south under the high wooden vaults, while trumpeters blared farewell from the balcony over the door to the great hall.

Sarah Bailey joined the slow-moving crowd, grateful that the first performance was over but afraid to go home, hearing what people said, but not caring whether they had liked it or not.

"Didn't you think the Doctor was hilarious? Let's hope the car doors aren't frozen shut."

"It was even better than last year. Jesus, it's a long walk to the parking lot."

"Oh, no, not half as good as last year. Oh, God, why didn't I wear my boots?"

"Why do they always have to kill poor old Saint George?"

"Oh, sir, you must allow me to instruct you. I think you will be interested to learn that among the Musurongo of the Congo the king is put to death on the first day of his reign."

Sarah was on the edge of exhaustion. She wanted to cry. Where in this enormous building was there a hole she could crawl into?

Pushing her way across the tide of people, she found her way to the steps leading upward to the balcony above the great hall. Halfway up she stopped. Below the balcony, on the floor of the enormous room, dozens of performers were changing into their street clothes, bundling up. The puppeteer covered his tall creations with a protective cloth. The Morris men laid out their sticks and swords in perfect order for tomorrow. Some of the children were sleepy and drooping, others raced around the hall.

Here on the stairs, neither up nor down, Sarah was alone. The tears she had feared might come, did come. She leaned on the railing and gave way.

"Sarah?" Someone spoke to her softly.

Sarah turned and looked down. Arlo Field was climbing up to her, still wearing the shirt of the Red Cross Knight.

At once Sarah knew what it was that had been missing in Morgan, what it was she had tried not to hunger for. It was Arlo, it was Arlo Field. He was a secret she had been keeping from herself. He was normalcy, he was common sense. He was clever and funny and kind. He was not twisted into a desperate knot of narcissism and suspicion and fear.

Sobbing, she held out her arms, and Arlo reached up and gathered her in, murmuring her name, knowing that this time she wasn't loving the whole world, she was loving him. It was his own face she was kissing and wetting with her tears.

If Morgan had seen them, if he had happened to look up the stairway and catch his wife in the arms of Arlo Field, it would have been like a bad movie—the wrathful husband opening the door at just the wrong moment, while the guilty couple sprang apart.

But if he did, they didn't know it. They clung together for only a few minutes, and then Sarah pulled away and wiped her face and glowed at Arlo and ran down the stairs.

Arlo changed his clothes in a lovesick daze. He almost forgot his camera, although the exposed film was waiting for him in the astronomy lab, with its image of forty-four suns in a giant figure eight above the roof of Memorial Hall. All he had to do now was remove it from the camera and dunk it in a tray of developer. Grinning to himself, he headed for the memorial corridor and the north door.

The Henshaws and the Beavers had come to the Revels together. The arrangements for the evening's entertainment had been made by Helen Henshaw, who was still trying to convince herself that life was perfectly normal, that her husband was not out of his mind, that he was only going through a rather peculiar phase.

"Oh, wasn't it grand?" she said, pulling on her gloves.

"The usual riotous success," said Ellery Beaver, winding his red scarf around his neck.

"Utterly delightful," said Margo Beaver, buttoning her coat.

Ernest Henshaw said nothing.

Ellery shouldered his way forward to walk beside his chief. "Oh, say, Ernest, did you hear the news? The General Counsel has determined that the overpass is definitely the property of the university. It's too bad. It means we've got to do something."

Henshaw glanced at him nervously and muttered, "Do something."

"Oh, Margo," said Helen, "I've been forgetting. I bought something for you. I've got it right here somewhere." She fumbled in her bag. "Look!" Triumphantly she produced the little snow scene, and shook it to make the white flakes fall around the jolly carolers, who stood in a row with their mouths open. "It's from that shop in the Holyoke Center. They've got ever so many more, from all over the world. You can have a real collection in your bedroom."

Margo was delighted. She took her new collectible and shook it. "Oh, how perfect. It's like a scene from *The Christmas Carol*."

"Are you sure we can't give you people a lift?" said Ellery Beaver.

"No, no, we'll just walk across the Common." Helen Henshaw wrapped her coat more tightly around her as they stepped out the door into a blast of icy wind. She glowered at her husband. "Ernest is such a great walker."

"Terrible night," said Ellery. He gave his boss a mock salute and went off with his wife in the direction of the parking garage, calling back over his shoulder, "One good thing . . . bitter night . . . tent city . . . throw in the towel . . . problem . . . become moot."

"What?" said Henshaw, and through the blizzard the words came back faintly, "Moot, I said moot."

There were no Dickensian carolers on the overpass as the Henshaws took a shortcut to the Common. Nor was the snow falling in feathery flakes as it did in the enclosed world of the little glass ball. It was coming down with a finespun violence that promised a heavy accumulation by morning. On the overpass the fabric walls of the tents billowed in the wind. A clumsy muffled shape swept snow from a sagging roof.

A tall, anxious-looking woman moved from tent to tent, putting her head inside to ask the same questions again and again: "Has anyone seen Gretchen? Where the hell is Maggody?"

The shortcut took Ernest and Helen Henshaw across Cambridge Common. Ernest hardly noticed the blowing snow. He was thinking once again about excess. He dared not look back as they approached the Civil War Memorial, because the dreaded procession of boxes was trailing after him, mounding up around him, engulfing him, threatening to block his way.

Nor did Helen concern herself with the real snow falling on the Common. As her fur-lined boots moved along the path, her vision was filled with the magical little scenes in the shop, the carolers, the snowmen, the laughing Santa Claus, the Christmas angel, the deer with her fawn. They were such perfect little worlds, so fanciful, so charming!

Therefore they both failed to see the snow-covered form of Maggody lying stiff and cold and lifeless at the foot of the memorial to the Union dead.

CHAPTER 32

Now bitter winter binds the earth
And whistling winds bring snow,
And New Year's Day is almost come
So Gawain now must go.
  "Sir Gawain and the Green Knight"

The shortest day was prelude to the longest night and the worst storm in a couple of years.

Sarah Bailey didn't learn about the death of Jeffery Peck until she and Morgan struggled through the snow all the way home to Maple Avenue. Then they had a phone call from Kevin Barnes, who had heard about it from his girlfriend, Chickie Pickett, who said the news was all over the Science Center.

For Sarah it was the final bursting of the boiler. Scalded, she turned furiously to Morgan and cried, "Where were you this afternoon? Where *were* you?"

Morgan was ready. He smiled at her. "What are you talking about? I was right here. I called you, remember? I couldn't find the graph paper." Then he showed her the work he had been doing, the population curves for the pied-billed grebe, and talked about his exciting new theory about diving ducks. He was tender and loving. He gathered her in his arms, and said how worried he had been about the stress she was under, and promised they would go somewhere when her work was done, somewhere sunny and warm. Then he brought up the ugly thing that had lain buried between them, the thing they never talked about.

"I'm sorry about the baby's dress," he said, murmuring into her hair, holding her close. "I've been under stress too, but it was a terrible thing to do." And then he took out of a drawer a new little piece of infant clothing. "Look," he said, showing her the Donald Duck embroidery on the front, "a pied-billed grebe."

As a peace offering it was so charming, Sarah's fears diminished. In bed with Morgan she lay quietly, her thoughts in turmoil, thinking about the violent deaths of Jeffery Peck and Tom Cobb and Henry Shady. Her doubts rose and fell, then rose again. But overwhelming her misery was her memory of the warm pressure of Arlo's lips and the tender embrace of his arms. Even with Morgan lying asleep beside her, she did not feel guilty. She lay in the dark staring at the window, watching the snow swirl around the streetlight—but every now and then she held her breath, hoping to feel a thump from the baby in her womb. There was none.

Mary and Homer Kelly were a long time getting home. It wasn't the awful driving that kept them out of bed, or the fact that Albert Maggody lay dead on Cambridge Common. They didn't know what had happened to Maggody. They were ignorant too of the death of Jeffery Peck. They were late because of their anxiety about the tent dwellers at Harvard Towers.

Arlo Field was with them as they pushed open the door of Memorial Hall and stopped short on the steps to take in the magnitude of what was happening.

"Those homeless people can't stay out in this," said Mary, "not tonight."

"Hell, no," said Homer. "Come on, let's get 'em out of there."

Arlo was still dizzy with the thought of Sarah. He had to force himself to remember the completed film waiting for him in his camera, the fulfillment of his year of work. "Right," he said, "but where can they go?"

"There are a couple of shelters," said Mary. "And, good Lord, what about Gretchen? We've got to find Gretchen first. She can't give birth in a tent in a snowstorm."

But when they put their heads inside the tents they found most of the people in Palmer Nifto's encampment already gone, including Gretchen.

The girl called Millie, one of the kids from Phillips Brooks House, was unplugging her coffeepot and pouring the coffee out into the snow. Her eyes were all that showed between hat and scarf. "Gretchen?" she said. "No, she hasn't been back."

Shelter, University Lutheran Church

"Maybe she's in Saint Elizabeth's, having her baby," said Mary hopefully.

"Nope," said Millie, "I called there. Nobody's seen her for a couple of days. Maggody's missing too."

Homer took the heavy pot from Millie. "Maggody too? My God."

Mary looked at Homer fiercely. She scowled at Arlo. "We've got to find them."

Blinding flurries of snow hurled themselves at the crevices between Homer's scarf and his neck and lodged in his hair and beard. He uttered a sepulchral laugh. "Well, goddamnit, of course we've got to find them."

"Me too," said Arlo. "I'll look too." He pulled his knitted hat down over his ears, mopped at his glasses, and tried to dismiss his camera from his mind.

They helped Millie carry her stuff back to Phillips Brooks House, and then they fanned out—Mary to Harvard Square and Homer to the Yard. Arlo's bailiwick was the subway entrances and train platforms and the levels where all the buses came and went.

It was no use. Gretchen Milligan and Albert Maggody were nowhere to be found.

At two in the morning, Homer and Mary met Arlo for coffee in an all-night bistro on JFK Street. They were stiff with cold. Their hats and coats were clotted with snow. Arlo warmed his hands on his coffee mug and passed along a piece of shocking news. In his exploration of the outbound subway platform he had run across a student of his, who had told him about Jeffery Peck's fall from a balcony at the Science Center.

"Jesus!" said Arlo. "Which balcony?" The student didn't know.

In the all-night café Homer and Mary were too numb to

do more than shake their heads in horror. The three of them sat wordlessly around the plastic table, crouched under the hideous glare of the fluorescent lights, sipped their coffee with blue lips, and went home to bed.

So it wasn't Homer or Mary or Arlo who found the dead body of old man Maggody. It was Palmer Nifto.

At three o'clock in the morning, while a snowplow clattered and banged along Garden Street, clearing the thoroughfare for the morning traffic, Palmer left his bar in Harvard Square and crossed Cambridge Common, pushing his rubber boots through the drifted snow, heading for his cozy office bedroom in Memorial Hall.

Palmer felt pleasantly lit, and warm as toast in the fur coat flapping around his knees. The coat was a lucky find from the secondhand bin of First Parish Unitarian. He had managed to get there right after a new batch of stuff came in.

Palmer's mind was hot and racing, making plans for the morrow. He would have missed the sight of old man Maggody if the flashing headlights of the snowplow had not flickered over the body stretched out in the snow at the foot of the Civil War Memorial. Then something at the side of his eye registered the familiar shape of *homeless-man-asleep,* and he stopped to take a look.

He knew at once that it was Maggody, and that Maggody was dead. There was a stiffness in the form under the blanket. The face was white with hoarfrost, the beard a nest of icicles. Palmer touched Maggody's old cheek, and his hand drew back. Maggody's face was cold as the bitter air.

It was painfully clear what must have happened. Maggody had shuffled away from the tent city, he had wandered in his aimless way across the intersection, clutching his blanket around him, and then, when he could go no

farther, he had lain down under the monument. And the cold had worked its way inward through the blanket and the thin clothing and the wrinkled old skin, and penetrated to Maggody's bones and vital organs and stopped his heart.

Something rose up in Palmer Nifto's breast, but it wasn't pity. He saw at once that Maggody's death was a sparkling opportunity, a gift from heaven. HOMELESS MAN FREEZES TO DEATH ON CAMBRIDGE COMMON—what a godsend!

Then, standing in the blowing snow looking down at Maggody, Palmer realized that he could do better than Cambridge Common. *Much* better than Cambridge Common.

It was a good thing the old man was so small and shriveled. Picking him up, Palmer was surprised at the lightness of his burden. He set off in the direction of Berkeley Street, hoping to meet no one on the way.

CHAPTER 33

> *What shall I give to the Child in the manger?*
> *What shall I give to the beautiful boy?*
> *Grapes I will give to him, hanging in clusters,*
> *Baskets of figs for the Child to enjoy.*
>
> Spanish carol

I f Gretchen Milligan had been a reader, she might have thought of herself as Hans Christian Andersen's Little Match Girl, who sat barefoot in the snow beside the rich man's house, envisioning the comfort and luxury within. Gretchen too was peering into someone's glowing windows, eager to know what was going on inside.

But the Little Match Girl had frozen to death in the cold. Gretchen was perfectly warm and comfortable. All through the afternoon and all night she holed up in the heated garage of the Henshaws' beautiful house on Berkeley Street.

Nor was she likely to starve like the Little Match Girl. Nestled on the plush upholstery of Ernest Henshaw's Mercedes, Gretchen nibbled on goodies baked by the nice ladies from the church—brownies and muffins and oatmeal cookies. She had taken a big bagful from their table at Harvard Towers.

Half sitting up because it was too uncomfortable to lie down, she lay snuggled in the cozy back seat with her baby bumping around inside her—playing basketball, it felt like.

Gretchen was happy in the Henshaws' garage. She didn't know who they were, but she felt close to them just the same, as though she were living their lives at second hand.

191

Sometimes she got out of the car and looked through the garage window into the window of the living room. There was also a clear view of the front door.

The mistress of the house had been at home all afternoon. Gretchen could see her now and then, moving from room to room. Once she stood at the window, and Gretchen ducked back out of sight. But the tall woman did not look out. She was unrolling some sort of fabric, trying it at the window, rolling it up again.

For a while Gretchen worried that somebody would come for one of the cars. They would open the garage door and find her there. But nobody did. And when the master and mistress of the house went out for the evening, they didn't take a car. They walked to the end of the street and turned the corner. Later on, Gretchen saw them returning the same way.

The night was really dark, except for the white snow, which kept falling like anything. Gretchen lay down on the back seat of the car and ate the crumbled pieces of another brownie. Then she brushed away the crumbs and went to sleep.

In the last month of pregnancy she always slept fitfully. At three-thirty in the morning it took only a small sound to jerk her awake—the click of the latch on the front gate.

Drowsily Gretchen heaved herself out of the back seat and went to the window. Oh, Jesus, who was that? A lumpy shape moved stealthily toward the front porch. It was a man carrying something over his shoulder.

Should she knock on the door between the garage and the kitchen and wake up the family? For a moment Gretchen had a vision worthy of the Little Match Girl—maybe they would thank her and take her inside and hug her and adopt her as their daughter and her baby as their grandchild. But Gretchen was too heavy, too sleepy. She couldn't summon the will to do anything but gaze out the window.

She saw the man creep up the steps and dump the thing he was carrying right against the door. The thing was a person. She watched as he rearranged the arms and legs, went down the steps, and turned to look back. At last he started up the walk, blowing on his hands.

Then he made his only mistake. He stopped to light a cigarette. Through the curtain of falling snow the glare of the burning match was like the mystical illumination of the matches in the hands of the Little Match Girl. For an instant it lighted up his face, and Gretchen knew at once who he was.

It was Palmer Nifto.

CHAPTER 34

When they bereaved his life so good,
The moon was turnèd into blood,
The earth and temple shaking stood,
And graves full wide did open.
　　　　　　Carol, "Wondrous Works"

It was a snow emergency in Cambridge. The city plows
had begun working in the middle of the night, but by
morning the cleared streets were once more inches
deep, and they had to start over.

The emergency line was jammed with complaints. People on streets lined with three-deckers complained that
Brattle Street always got the best service, and when were
they going to plow Aberdeen Avenue? *I got to get to work,*
the kids are hungry, I need milk for the baby. We been waiting
all morning, where the hell are you?

The callers from Brattle Street said there was entirely too
much political correctness in the Public Works Department,
which was ignoring the needs of the property owners who
paid the highest taxes. *And, please, would you kindly avoid*
leaving a mountain of snow at the end of my driveway?

Ernest Henshaw did not call the Public Works Department. Nor did he call the police to say that there was a
dead man on his doorstep. When he put on his coat and
hat and galoshes and opened the front door, expecting to
slog through the snow to Harvard Yard, he was stopped
cold by the obstacle that lay across his path.

He stared down in shocked surprise at the body of Maggody, and for several moments he did not move or speak.

Then, very quietly, he closed the door, slipped down

the hall, and descended softly into the cellar to hide behind the furnace. He remained there the rest of the morning. His wife Helen sat at her desk riffling through sample books of wallpaper and upholstery fabric, picking out favorites, telephoning the wholesalers for ten rolls of this and a dozen yards of that. She had no idea her husband was still at home.

But Ernest Henshaw was too shaken to budge. The body on his doorstep was yet another piece of excess. It was like a bulky object delivered by UPS. He wanted no part of it, no part of it at all.

Therefore, when Palmer Nifto came back to his command tent at Harvard Towers and swept the snow off the roof and burrowed inside to watch the noontime news, he was dismayed that there was no scandalized report about Maggody. The jocular guy on the screen chattered about a couple of drug arrests and the latest loss by the Boston Celtics. Turning solemn for a moment before droning through the no-school announcements, he mentioned the death of Jeffery Peck. But he did not purse his lips in sorrow and announce that a poor old homeless man had frozen to death on the doorstep of Harvard's Vice-President for Government and Community Affairs.

Angrily Palmer switched off the set and hurried back to Berkeley Street, hardly bothering to greet his fellow protesters as they drifted back to Harvard Towers in twos and threes.

Gretchen Milligan, peering out the window of the Henshaws' garage, saw Nifto standing across the street staring at the front porch. The poor dead person was still there. She didn't know what it all meant—why Palmer had dumped the person there in the first place, why no one had done anything about it, and why Palmer had come back to the scene of the crime.

She didn't really care. She was having too good a time playing with all the perks in the Mercedes. Where was the key? It wasn't in the glove compartment. Gretchen soon found it under the carpet on the driver's side. At once she pushed it into the ignition and turned it one click. There! Now she could try the tape deck, inserting one cassette after another from the bin in the dashboard. But the tapes weren't Gretchen's kind of music. Oh, it was okay for these rich people to like classical music, but it always sounded the same to Gretchen, so she turned on the radio to her favorite heavy-metal station, very softly, and lay down on the back seat to listen, reaching into her bag of brownies, feeling the baby lurch inside her. *Oh, ouch.*

The storm was over. The sun was out, bright and clear in the blue sky, casting bold blue shadows on the dazzling white snow in the Henshaws' front yard as Palmer Nifto stopped to stare at it from across the street. Knobs and domes of snow lay on the foundation planting around the front porch.

Shit! The fucking body was still there.

Standing on the corner of Berkeley Street and Phillips Place, Palmer took only a few minutes to decide what to do. He'd make an anonymous phone call to the office of the Dean of the Episcopal Divinity School, which was right around the corner. "I'm afraid the person is dead," he would say gravely. "I rang the bell, but I couldn't rouse the occupants, and I have an emergency in my place of business, so I'm calling from work. Perhaps you could send someone over to take a look?"

The stratagem worked perfectly. "Good heavens," said

the scandalized Dean of EDS. "Thank you very much for calling. I'll take a look right away." In his excitement he failed to asked who was calling, hung up, threw on his coat, and ran across the street.

Good Lord, there *was* a body on the Henshaws' front porch. The Dean knelt over it, lifted back the blanket, and looked in horror at the dead face of Albert Maggody. A homeless man, obviously it was an old homeless man. The poor soul had hoped to find refuge from the cold in the warm house of Harvard's Vice-President for Government and Community Affairs, but Henshaw had turned him away.

Grimly the Dean rang the bell. At once Helen Henshaw came to the door and jerked it open, then started back in surprise at the sight of the body of Maggody. She gaped at the Dean. "What on earth? Who's this?"

"I'm afraid this man has frozen to death on your doorstep," said the Dean, not without a feeling of reproachful satisfaction. "A homeless man, I think. Perhaps you'd better call the police."

"But he can't have been here long. Ernest would have seen him when he left for work." Then a suspicion dawned on Helen. Turning away from the Dean, she cried, "ERNEST?"

There was a muffled thump in the cellar. Helen abandoned the Dean and the dead man at the door, ran down the hall, threw open the cellar door, and called loudly, "Ernest, are you down there?"

Sheepishly Ernest Henshaw emerged from behind the furnace and followed his wife upstairs. In shaking fury Helen spoke to the Dean, who was still standing in the open door, silhouetted against the sunlit snow. "Won't you come in and shut the door? I suppose we have to leave the—the body just where it is without disturbing it."

"No, thank you," said the Dean. "I won't come in. I'll just stand here and watch beside the poor old soul."

Why this remark should have inflamed Helen's anger is a mystery. She was about to say something sharp when there was a scream from the garage.

Ernest Henshaw's instinct to vanish from the face of the earth was a good one, but the vultures of the press soon found him and tore at his bowels.

"Is it true, Mr. Henshaw, that your office of Government and Community Affairs has failed to respond to the pleas of the homeless community camped out on Harvard property in the bitter cold? Is it also true that you failed to open your own door to this pitiful old man, with the result that he froze to death on your front porch? Is it also a fact that a homeless teenager gave birth in your garage?"

Well, it was superb. Palmer Nifto was delighted. There it was on the national news, the grim follow-up to the hilarious sofa story of the day before. In ecstasy Palmer watched the camera zoom in on the body on the doorstep, with joy he gazed at Ernest Henshaw blanching and stuttering at the camera and Ellery Beaver blustering in his office in Massachusetts Hall, his boiled eyes bulging.

Of course it wasn't true about Gretchen Milligan. Her baby was born in Saint Elizabeth's Hospital, not in the Henshaws' garage. When a scandalized Helen Henshaw discovered Gretchen in Ernest's Mercedes, shrieking in the throes of childbirth, she simply called a taxi and popped her into it, thus rescuing from unspeakable abominations the clean cushions of the car.

When the news began spreading among the members of
the Revels cast on Saturday that the old black man at Harvard Towers had frozen to death during the night, Mary
and Homer Kelly were dressing in the great hall for the afternoon performance. They looked at each other grimly
and swore, and Mary quoted William Blake. "It puts all
Heaven in a rage."

"Right you are," said Homer gloomily. "I guess Heaven
was occupied with something more important last night."

And that was the trouble, thought Mary. There had
been no rage at all. Everyone had let the matter drift.

None of them had seen it, that Maggody was the crux,
the center, the hub around which the world should have
been turning. Harvard University should have fixed its
multitudinous clever eye on Maggody. He should have
been the object of scholarly study, of laboratory investigation, of mighty decisions by the President and Fellows and
the Faculty of Arts and Sciences and the Board of Over-
seers. All the professors in all the learned disciplines, all
the assistant professors and associates, all the teachers of
syntactic typology and Chinese historiography and exposi-
tory writing should have dropped their lecture notes and
abandoned their blackboards and blue books and rushed
to Maggody's aid. It was an appalling and general failure
of imagination and justice and pity.

Mary took her long gown off the rack and greeted Arlo
Field. "Hello there, Saint George." With a touch of accusa-
tion in her voice she said, "I must say, you're looking aw-
fully cheerful."

"I am?" Arlo tried to wipe the grin from his face. A ray
from the stained-glass window at the west end of the
enormous room made a purple blotch on his nose.

Homer Kelly too was looking at him soberly. "Look here,

Arlo, do you know which balcony Jeff fell from?" Homer disappeared for an instant as he pulled on his Father Christmas robe. When his head popped out again, he said, "What was he doing in the Science Center anyway? He wasn't a scientist, was he? I thought he was some kind of historian."

"He fell from my balcony, I'm afraid." Arlo buckled the belt of his Red Cross shirt. "Somebody saw him on the way down. I wasn't there, but it was my fault that all the doors were open. I don't know what the hell he was doing in our lab."

"Homer?" said Mary Kelly. Her psychological analysis on the subject of jealousy and its deadly ramifications had mushroomed during the night. It didn't worry her that she had never studied the works of Sigmund Freud and knew nothing about criminal psychosis. After all, some things were obvious to anyone with a grain of common sense. She had been brooding about it all morning while helping Homer dig out the car. Sitting tensely beside him as they wallowed through the woods and skidded out onto Route 2 and plunged in the direction of Cambridge, she perfected her theory. Had Homer noticed, for instance—?

But Homer was gone. He was running down the length of the great hall to help the set designer manhandle a collapsing piece of scenery. At the other end of the enormous room a little girl fell off a table and began to howl. "Oh, well, never mind," said Mary, looking sorrowfully at Arlo as he hopped on one foot, pulling on his long black hose.

Arlo grinned back, then tried to compose his expression to hide the glee he felt, in spite of the deaths of Jeffery Peck and that poor old homeless guy, and goddamnit, in spite of the failure of his year-long effort to capture the analemma on film.

Well, it had been sickening, his first look at the negative. This morning he had at last removed the film holder from his camera and dropped the negative into a tray of developer and then into hypo, and turned on the light to take a look. At once the forty-four suns were visible, thank God, making a lopsided figure eight, and the exposure for getting the tower of Memorial Hall in the foreground had turned out just right, but—Christ!—what was that pale blob in the foreground?

Arlo's heart sank. What did it mean, another whole year before he could get a decent result? He hung up the negative to dry and emerged gloomily from the darkroom to find Harley Finch staring at him.

"Well?" said Harley. "How did it come out?"

"Don't know yet," mumbled Arlo. "Have to make a print."

But even this blow had not destroyed the happiness that had kept him awake last night while the blizzard raged outside and the snowplows clanked and rattled along Huron Avenue. "Have you seen Sarah?" he asked Mary Kelly.

"No, not yet."

"She must be here somewhere," said Arlo dreamily, and he went off to look for her.

Mary gazed after him, making another instant psychiatric appraisal, feeling a little smug about her gift for probing the depths of human nature. It was too bad her husband, Homer, wasn't more aware of this kind of thing. Oh, of course, he was terrifically well informed about all sorts of areas of scholarly knowledge. He knew everything there was to know about the literary movements of nineteenth-century America, he was familiar with the social and scientific revolutions of the time, he was a Thoreau scholar of distinction, and in criminal investigation he had a genius for pouncing on the truth. But in understanding the springs of human motivation the poor man was just another meatball.

◇   ◇   ◇   ◇   ◇   ◇   ◇   ◇   ◇   ◇   ◇   ◇

PART FIVE

THE LAMENT

Behold, behold, what have I done?
I cut him down like the evening sun.
  Traditional British Mummers' Play

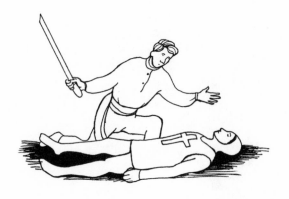

◇   ◇   ◇   ◇   ◇   ◇   ◇   ◇   ◇   ◇   ◇   ◇

CHAPTER 35

They bound Christ's body to a tree,
And wounded him full sore;
From every wound the blood ran down,
Till Christ could bleed no more. . . .
                    Carol, "The Lamb of God"

There were scraping sounds below the window. Someone was shoveling the walk. Sarah looked down and saw Chickie Pickett dump a shovelful of snow to one side.

"Oh, Morgan, Chickie's down there shoveling. Don't you want to help?"

Morgan was at his desk. He didn't look up. "Oh, I think she can handle it."

Sarah looked at the intent curve of his back. This morning all her doubts had returned to torment her. She sat on the edge of the bed and pulled on her boots. "Are you coming, Morgan? We'll be late if we don't hurry."

Still he did not look up. "You go ahead. I'll be along shortly. There's something I've got to do first."

"Well, all right." Feeling a terrible certainty, Sarah clumped down the stairs alone, and stopped on the front walk to thank Chickie.

"No problem," said Chickie, her face rosy in the cold.

Left to himself, Morgan jumped up and went to the window. Sarah was heading for Inman Square to take the bus. Good. He would dodge over to Kirkland Street and run the whole way and get to Mem Hall first. Morgan snatched up his coat, pulled open his desk drawer, and put something in his pocket.

205

His mood was triumphant, frenzied. He felt excited, a little crazy. But that was Sarah's doing. It was Sarah who was driving him insane. She was incorrigible. Getting rid of one fucker, what good did that do? There was always another. Arlo Field! He should have seen all along that it was Arlo Field!

The sharpness of the cold struck Morgan's face, and he thrust his chin down into his parka. Chickie had finished clearing the walk. It was a bright day, with the sun smashing down on the heaps of snow thrown up by the plow. Morgan strode to the end of Maple Avenue, then zigzagged over to Kirkland and ran all the way to Memorial Hall, slipping on the icy cracked concrete, nearly falling, regaining his balance, and running on again.

He entered by the north door to find the place already jumping. The memorial corridor was full of cheerful people, waiting to get into Sanders Theatre. Most of them had children clinging to them or hopping up and down beside them, because it was a Saturday-afternoon performance. Now the thick crowd began funneling into Sanders, handing their tickets to Dotty and Linda, Spencer and Robbie, who stood by the two sets of stairs. "Up one flight to the mezzanine," said Linda. "Through the door to Row B," said Spencer.

The building manager looked out from the door to his office and said hello to Morgan. "How did it go last night?"

"Oh, fine," said Morgan, but he could remember nothing about last night, nothing about his leaping and stamping with the Morris dancers, only his relief at the absence of Jeffery Peck, and then the revival of his agony as he stood watching at the bottom of the stairs while Sarah fell into the arms of Arlo Field.

Slipping into the great hall, he hurried up to the table allotted to the Morris men. The hall was full of people in every state of undress. At one end the chorus had gathered in a ring to practice the "Sussex Mummers' Carol"—

> *God bless the mistress of this house,*
> *With gold chain round her breast;*
> *Where-e'er her body sleeps or wakes,*
> *Lord send her soul to rest.*

Morgan looked around for the other Morris dancers. A couple of them were talking to the puppeteer, helping him uncover his tall mannikins and lift them high. But no one stood at the table where the swords and sticks and bells had been laid down in perfect order. Morgan chose one of the swords and slipped it under his coat.

He took it to the hallway beside the men's room. No one was going in or out. No one saw him slip into the broom closet, pull the light string, and close the door.

The closet was crowded with cleaning equipment, a set tub, a mop bucket, and a waxing machine. Morgan took the whetstone out of his pocket, held it under the faucet, and began sharpening the sword. It was slow work. Skillfully he drew the blade across the stone, sharpening the entire edge at each stroke. Now and then he turned the sword over and worked on the other side. He did not tire. He kept on and on, testing the edge now and then with his finger until at last the blade drew blood.

Once again Sanders Theatre was jammed with jiggling people. By two-thirty there was a high excited noise in the big chamber, with everybody talking at once, leaning over the backs of benches, hailing friends across the hall, standing up, sitting down, rearranging coats, and telling one an-

other it was too hot or too cold. Every ticket had been sold, but a bunch of the homeless people from Harvard Towers had filtered past the ticket-takers. They were sitting here and there, wherever there were empty seats.

Polite Cambridge type in Eddie Bauer padded vest (mail-order credit-card classic): "Oh, sorry, but I think that's my seat. Look, my ticket says D4."

Bob Chumley in Morgan Memorial mackinaw, la Mode Hobo: "Well, Jesus, you're late, like I thought it would be okay."

For some of the smaller children it was their first theatrical experience. They were squealing and crawling over their parents, unaware that the dark hollow stage was about to be transformed into a place of magic.

Even for the adults it was pleasant to be embraced by the warm enclosing space, to breathe the golden air and admire the playfulness of the architecture and enjoy the nineteenth-century atmosphere of tawny wood and cast-iron column. Who had thickened it but eminences from the past, like Oliver Wendell Holmes and Ralph Waldo Emerson and Charles Eliot Norton and Winston Churchill and Professor John Finley and T. S. Eliot, speaking from the stage, standing between the stone figures of James Otis and Josiah Quincy at either side?

Otis and Quincy were still there, pale as milk in their Carrara marble, looking impassively down, while the squinting animal faces above the stage stared outward at the mezzanine. At the back of the stage the painted Harvard coat of arms declared the virtue of VERITAS, and high above, only dimly visible, were a thousand square feet of Latin inscriptions. The sumptuous words had been meant to inspire the young with the generosity of the forefathers in erecting this building for the cultivation of the highest arts and the instruction of succeeding generations.

Well, here they were, the succeeding ages, waiting to be entertained, eager only for the bright revelry to come, unconscious of any call to generosity and sacrifice.

It was Arlo Field who provided the sacrifice. After the jolly horn prelude and the processional entry of the chorus singing its way down the aisles, after Walt's invitation to everyone to join in "The First Nowell," after the Morris men performed their stick dance—with Kevin Barnes filling in again for Jeffery Peck—after the children's street games and the ceremonial parade with the boar's head, after Saint George's mock battle with the dragon and the second entry of the Morris men—after all these festive rites were over, it was Arlo's turn to enter the mystic center of the sword dance and become the symbolic victim—like Dr. Box's Adonis, whose bones were ground in a mill, and Osiris, who was killed and revived with the growing wheat, and John Barleycorn, who was crushed between two stones.

While the concertina played its merry tune, the Morris dancers raised their swords and executed their intricate figures and tramped around Saint George. Once more they wove their steely web around him, and then—*snick!*—the swords were snatched away, and light flashed along the edge of one blue blade, and Arlo fell with blood streaming from his throat.

CHAPTER 36

Out of children eleven I've got but seven
And they be started up to heaven,
Out of the seven I've got but five,
And they be starved to death alive;
Out of the five I've got but three,
And they be popped behind a tree;
Out of the three I've got but one,
And he got around behind the sun.
Traditional British Mummers' Play

Hastily, silently, in a hush of horror, they picked up Arlo and carried him offstage. The audience was silent too, awestruck and bewildered. What had happened? For a moment the stage was empty, and then Walt came forward and explained. His face was white.

"There's been an accident. I'm afraid we'll have to cancel the rest of the performance."

There was a general groan. Walt held up his hands. "There'll be an extra performance on the thirtieth of December. Substitute tickets will be handed out at the doors as you leave."

Disappointed men and women rose from their seats, children whimpered, twelve hundred people poured into the memorial corridor. *What happened? Someone was hurt. It was those goddamn swords, my God!*

There was chaos at the ticket desk. *The new date's no good, we'll be away, so may we come tomorrow?* At the other end of the corridor there was a blockage, where a pair of medical technicians eased a stretcher out the door.

In the great hall Homer Kelly blew his stack. "Who the hell?" he bellowed. "Who the hell was holding the god-damned bloody sword?" Because there it was, piled up with the rest on the table, its razor edge gleaming, Arlo Field's blood dripping off it like the blood of a chicken from a kitchen knife.

The Morris men didn't know. In their consternation at the sight of Arlo lying on the floor with his throat cut, they had dropped their swords in horror.

In his jolly red Father Christmas robe, Homer thundered at them, "My God, you were all wearing gloves? Why the hell were you wearing gloves?"

They looked at each other sheepishly, and Bill Foose spoke up. "It's Joan. She does the costumes. She said gloves and red sashes. Green baldrics. You know."

For a moment Homer stared at the six of them, facing him in a row. Then Sarah Bailey joined them. Her face was red and swollen. She had been sobbing her heart out in the ladies' room at the bottom of the steep stairway beside Sanders Theatre.

"Well, tell me," said Homer, "could it have been an accident?" Avoiding the bloody sword, he picked up one of the others. "All the rest have dull edges. They're not meant to be sharp, are they?" Homer turned to Morgan Bailey. "What would you do if you wanted to sharpen it? Use some kind of knife-sharpener?"

Morgan shrugged uneasily, and Kevin Barnes answered instead. "If it was me, I'd use a whetstone." He made a scraping gesture to show what he meant. "You just run it along the edge like this. Then you turn the sword over and do the other side."

Bernard Fox looked doubtful. "It would take you a while."

"Sure, but it would work."

Bernard looked at Homer darkly. "I suppose you think it

was one of us, right? I mean, you used to be this big detective, isn't that right?"

Homer flapped his hands. "I don't know what the hell I think. After all, somebody else could have sharpened the sword beforehand, and then one of you just picked it up and—"

"But you wouldn't be able to, you know, cut his throat with it," said Kevin, demonstrating, holding his neck, "unless you really meant to do it. You know, unless you really, like, slashed at him with what-do-you-call-it, malice aforethought."

Homer grimaced and changed the subject. "Now, listen. I hate to be the one to mention it, but this makes four— four people hurt—or worse—during this year's Revels. The police aren't going to think it's a coincidence. Henry Shady was killed in a traffic accident. Jeffery Peck died in a fall at the Science Center. Twenty-two witnesses saw him strike the glass roof of the cafeteria at two minutes after three o'clock yesterday afternoon. I'm sure the police will want to know what each of you was doing at the time." Homer hauled up his red robe and pulled a piece of paper out of his pocket. It was a list of sources for arsenate of lead. "Tom Cobb died after eating a candy bar into which arsenate of lead had been injected. Tell me, do any of you work with stained glass?"

They looked at him blankly.

"Or battery plates?" said Homer. "No? Ammunition? Metal roof sheeting? Lead-paint removal?"

Shuddering, Sarah moved away and went looking for Walt, the Old Master, to ask him to take Arlo's place as Saint George. But she couldn't pull herself together. She found Mary Kelly instead and fell weeping on her shoulder.

"I know," said Mary. And of course she did know. She

had guessed that a heavy connection had been building up between Arlo and Sarah. No wonder Sarah couldn't stop crying.

But Mary didn't know the other reason. It was something Sarah had remembered about Morgan—he kept a whetstone in his desk drawer. It was just a rectangle of hard gray stone for keeping the knives sharp, so they would cut cleanly, making delicate slices of cucumbers and tomatoes, slitting the meat of a chicken away from the bone, or slicing open the bodies of Morgan's specimen waterfowl.

The whetstone that had sharpened the sword that had cut Arlo's throat was Morgan's own. He had killed Henry Shady and Tom Cobb and Jeffery Peck. Sarah's doubts were gone forever.

CHAPTER 37

Then on the cross hangèd I was,
Where a spear to my heart did glance;
There issued forth both water and blood,
To call my true love to the dance.
Carol, "My Dancing Day"

It was a routine case of hypothermia. The pathologist at Massachusetts General Hospital looked dispassionately at the thawing body of Albert Maggody lying on his metal table. There was nothing exceptional about it at all. It was the cadaver of an aged African-American male exposed to conditions of extreme cold by the criminal carelessness of the city of Cambridge and Harvard University, and most likely God.

"Undress him, will you?" he said to his assistant, turning away to collect his instruments.

"Certainly," said the assistant. One by one she removed Maggody's cracked shoes and his worn socks, trousers, and underwear. Then she unbuttoned his sweater. As she pulled the sleeve over the closed fist of his right hand, something fell out and fluttered to the floor. It was a piece of paper wrinkled into a ball.

The assistant picked it up and tossed it in the wastebasket. "No, wait, let me see it," said the pathologist.

Clucking her tongue, she picked up the wadded piece of paper and handed it to him. He pulled it open and read it silently. The first part was in pencil—

Darling,
Meet me at three o'clock?
I love you.*
                    Sarah
*Passionately!

The second part had been added with a typewriter—

*JEFFERY, MAKE IT TOMORROW
IN THE ASTRONOMY LAB.*

Puzzled, he looked up at his assistant. "The cadaver in the next room, what's his name? It's Jeffery, isn't it? Jeffery with an 'e' in the wrong place? What's this old geezer doing with a letter addressed to Jeffery?"

The assistant shrugged her shoulders. "Only connection I can see, they both came over from Cambridge Hospital."

"Right, the same hospital. And they must have died within an hour or two of each other. And the Cambridge Common, where this old guy froze to death, isn't far from the Science Center, where the other guy fell and broke his neck. A stone's throw away, so to speak."

"My, my, aren't we the great detective this morning? What else do you deduce, Mr. Holmes?"

"Oh, hell, it's nothing to me." The pathologist pocketed the piece of paper, then inserted his knife in Maggody's torso and slit it open with a single stroke. "Just a couple more Christmas cadavers."

But as he worked, he made up his mind to call the Cambridge Police. They might just possibly be interested in the coincidence about the letter.

◇ ◇ ◇ ◇ ◇ ◇ ◇ ◇ ◇ ◇ ◇ ◇

PART SIX

THE DOCTOR

A doctor! a doctor!
Is there a doctor to be found
Can quickly raise my noble son
Lies bleeding on the ground?
    Saint George and the Dragon

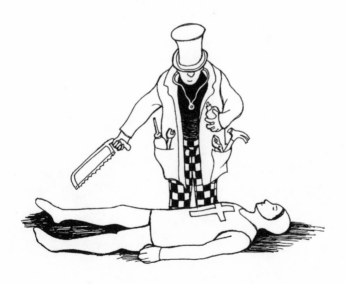

◇ ◇ ◇ ◇ ◇ ◇ ◇ ◇ ◇ ◇ ◇ ◇

CHAPTER 38

Now the green blade riseth from the buried grain,
Wheat that in dark earth many days has lain;
Love lives again, that with the dead has been. . . .
                    Carol, "Love Is Come Again"

Kevin Barnes and Chickie Pickett were having lunch in the Greenhouse, the Science Center cafeteria, which had started serving meals again. The smashed glass roof had been covered with plywood. The cashier had done her best to cheer the place up by fastening a small aluminum Christmas tree to the top of her cash register. Her earrings were tiny Christmas balls.

"How is he?" said Chickie, dabbing at her eyes.

Kevin made a *this way, that way* gesture with his hand. "It's touch-and-go. Sarah spent the night in the waiting room of the Intensive Care Unit. She says they just shake their heads whenever she asks how he is."

"Oh," sobbed Chickie, "he can't die, he just can't."

"What's the matter?" said Kevin. "You like him better than me?"

Chickie knew he was just kidding. She gave him an affectionate poke, teetered off on her high heels to the elevator, and ascended to the astronomy lab on the eighth floor.

Harley Finch was there, bumbling about. "Too bad about the analemma," he said, sounding a little smug.

"Too bad?"

"There's a big blot on the negative. See for yourself. He left it drying in the darkroom. One of his last acts," added Harley, with mortuary relish.

Chickie hurried into the darkroom, turned on the lamp,

219

plucked the negative from the drying line, and held it up to the light. Oh, shit, Harley was right. The suns were there, and the tower of Mem Hall, but there was a big white blotch on the bottom of the film.

Wait a minute. Chickie stared at the blotch. It wasn't altogether formless. She snapped off the darkroom light, laid the negative in the holder on the enlarger stand, slipped a sheet of photographic paper out of an envelope, and adjusted the focus to form an image. Patiently she counted twenty seconds. At last she snatched up the paper and slid it into a pan of developer. Bending over the pan she watched the image darken, and suppressed a squeal of surprise.

The blotch was not a blotch. It was a couple of men on the terrace, and one was heaving the other up on the railing. The two men were a little out of focus, but there was no mistaking who they were.

In Cambridge Hospital, Dr. Box asked the whereabouts of the Intensive Care Unit, then took the elevator to the fourth floor. There she was interrogated by the woman at the reception desk.

"You wish to see Mr. Field? Only family visitors are allowed. He has seen his mother, and no one else." The receptionist made a face. Arlo's mother had been a disaster. "Are you a relative?"

"I am his great-aunt," lied Dr. Box, gripping the straps of her briefcases.

"Well, you can wait in the hall if you like. He's in Compartment C. The nurse may let you in, but then again, she may not."

Dr. Box hurried down the hall and looked through the window of Compartment C.

Ah! There was the boy, flat on his back. His eyes were closed. He was white and still. There were tubes going in and out of him and padded bandages around his neck.

Dr. Box knocked on the window and raised her eyebrows at the nurse, who was hanging a bottle of red liquid on a hook and fastening it into a plastic hose.

The nurse looked at her, distraught, and shook her head, but Dr. Box wasn't having any of *that*. She knocked again, *rat-a-tat-tat*.

Impatiently the nurse came to the door, opened it a crack, and said, "He can't see anyone. He's lost a lot of blood. He's very ill."

"But I am his great-aunt."

"I'm *sorry*," said the nurse, and shut the door.

Dr. Box did not withdraw. She pressed her nose against the window and watched the nurse's every move. At last, with a *Get lost* gesture at Dr. Box, the nurse hurried off to care for another patient.

At once Dr. Box opened the door and nipped inside the compartment. Reaching into one of the bags dangling from her shoulders, she extracted a sprig of holly and approached Arlo's bedside. Gently she laid it on the white sheet over his chest. Then, smiling to herself, she closed her bag and went away.

Arlo opened his eyes.

The overworked intensive-care nurse was thoroughly disgusted. The mother of the man whose life they were trying to save had almost killed him by throwing her arms around his neck and starting a small hemorrhage. Then there had been the tired-looking young woman who had spent the entire night in the waiting room, but at least she had shown the courtesy of not trying to push her way in, like the madwoman in the purple hat. Now here was this ridiculous girl in the fuzzy fake-fur coat pounding on the glass, shaking a big envelope, and demanding to be let in.

Heaving a sigh, the nurse put her head out the door and said, "What are you, his second cousin once removed?"

"What?" Chickie Pickett flapped her envelope at the nurse. "He's got to see!"

"I'm sorry," said the nurse sarcastically, "but he can't see anything. He just happens to be fighting for his life."

But Arlo lifted his head and croaked at Chickie, "Show me!"

"Oh, the analemma's there, all right," cried Chickie, pushing past the nurse. "Like it looks just great. But there's this other stuff going on. Look." She pulled out the print she had made from Arlo's negative. It was still damp, but the picture was sharp and clear, the bright suns in the dark sky, the sunlit tower of Memorial Hall, and the violent action in the foreground. "It's two guys, two guys fighting up there on the porch—you know, the terrace. It's Morgan Bailey, and he's pushing Jeffery Peck over the railing. Sarah's husband, he killed Jeffery Peck! It's right here!"

Arlo focused his eyes on the print for a moment, then dropped his head back and closed his eyes.

"You see?" said the nurse. "I told you. Please leave at once."

But Arlo lifted his head again, and whispered, "Homer, call Homer Kelly."

"Homer Kelly? You mean that big guy with, like"— Chickie waggled her fingers excitedly under her chin— "whiskers?"

Arlo summoned a last effort from his vocal cords and wheezed. "Concord, he lives in Concord," then dropped his head again and closed his eyes.

Chickie leaned her furry bosom over him and kissed him while the furious nurse tugged at her coat.

Afterward the nurse went straight to her supervisor and demanded that visitors to Intensive Care be screened more thoroughly. "What about making them fill out a questionnaire? I mean—God!—I'm supposed to be responsible for saving these people's lives, and you should just *see* what goes on around here."

"Oh, pooh," said the supervisor. "Relax, honey. Take a day off. You're working too hard."

CHAPTER 39

Then woe is me,
Poor child for thee!
And ever mourn and say,
For thy parting
Nor say nor sing,
By, by, lullay, lullay!
"The Coventry Carol"

After her long night of drowsing in the waiting room of the Intensive Care Unit at Cambridge Hospital, Sarah was still painfully alarmed, and no one had set her mind at ease. She did not go home. Instead she ate breakfast in the Square, then went back to Memorial Hall to work with the Old Master.

Walt was taking Arlo's place. No one could be a better substitute, but he had to learn all of Saint George's lines, and he had to be told where to stand and how to move from place to place. Joan Hill was there to measure him for a new costume and whip it up in a hurry for the Sunday-afternoon performance. Homer Kelly had to leave a student conference a little early, in order to practice the resurrection scene with Walt and the Doctor and the Fool, but of course the student was grateful. She snatched up her notebook and charged out of the building.

Mary came in as she ran out. The student shouted, "Merry Christmas, Mrs. Kelly," and Mary laughed and wished her a happy new year.

Homer looked at his wife soberly. "Any news?"

She shook her head. "Nobody seems to know."

Solemnly they made their way upstairs and pushed through the thick horde of people in the corridor, and entered the great hall. But before Sarah Bailey could start her last-minute rehearsal, another crisis erupted.

"Hey, Sarah," said Kevin Barnes, "where's Morgan?" Kevin was dressed in his white trousers and red sash, and his bells jingled at his knees. In only twenty minutes the Morris men were supposed to go onstage for the first time. From the corridor Sarah could hear the pandemonium of twelve hundred people talking and calling to friends across the hall, and the noise of excited children and then the diminishing of the racket as everyone began pouring into Sanders Theatre.

Sarah didn't know where Morgan was. She had been afraid to go home. Her world had burst into fragments, she had found her treasure and lost it, and she was overwhelmed by the sense of continuing tragedy. "Find someone else," she said quickly. "There must be someone. Hurry, hurry."

"Well, Jesus," said Kevin, "who else is there?" He wandered off, feeling hopeless, but at once he ran into an old friend, Buck Zemowski, and his troubles were over. Buck had been the original Father Christmas before he came down with the flu, before Sarah dragooned Homer Kelly to take his place.

Grinning, Kevin brought him back to Sarah. "Guess what? We're in luck. Buck's the best Morris dancer in Boston."

Buck smiled modestly and demonstrated his prowess by leaping into the air and coming down with a crash.

"Well, that's wonderful," said Sarah.

"Come on, Buck, we'll get you decked out."

As it turned out, Morgan Bailey's clogs were a trifle small for Buck, but he suffered good-naturedly through the exertions of the afternoon, then went home and soaked his sore feet in a pan of soapy water.

"Where have you been?" said Morgan.

Sarah was too tired to make the obvious retort, "Well, where have *you* been?" She closed the door and went directly to Morgan's desk and opened the drawer.

The whetstone was missing. The middle drawer of Morgan's desk was neat, as usual, with everything in its own space—the sharpened pencils, the drafting tools, the calculator, the rolls of tape, the protractor and triangles, the collection of household tools, the hammer, the pliers, the screwdriver. But the little compartment reserved for Morgan's whetstone was empty.

Behind her back she could feel him watching her. Lately he was always watching her, he never took his eyes off her. Sometimes she wanted to scream at him to look at something else. *Look at your geese, look at your ducks, look at the great auk. Stop looking at Sarah Bailey.*

"What do you want in my desk?" said Morgan softly.

Silently Sarah looked at him. Then she turned back to the desk to pick up the ringing phone, aware that Morgan was reaching at the same time for the one that hung on the wall.

"Mrs. Bailey?"

"This is Sarah Bailey."

"Sergeant Hasty here, Cambridge Police. I wonder if you know anything about a certain letter, which I would like to read to you."

Sarah stared at the map of bird migration that hung over Morgan's desk, while Sergeant Hasty cleared his throat and read the words passed along to him by the pathologist at Massachusetts General Hospital.

"The first part is in pencil, and it goes like this." In a monotone Hasty read it aloud—"*Darling, Meet me at three o'clock? I love you.* And it's signed, *Sarah.* And there's a word at the bottom." Sergeant Hasty's voice flattened still further as he read the postscript: *"Passionately!"*

Sarah did not turn around, but she could feel Morgan's eyes on her back. "How—" she began. "I mean, where did the letter come from?"

"Wait a minute, there's more. This part is typed—*Jeffery, make it tomorrow in the astronomy lab.* Now, tell me, Mrs. Bailey, do you know anything about this letter?"

Yes, of course she knew something about the letter. She knew everything about the letter. It was the note she had written to Morgan last week. And there in front of her on Morgan's desk was the typewriter with which he must have added the rest. Somehow he had delivered it to Jeffery Peck, and then he had met Jeffery in the Science Center and tossed him over the railing.

"Mrs. Bailey, are you still there?"

"Yes, yes, I'm here." Dizzily Sarah leaned on the desk as everything fell into place, revelation beyond revelation, the waters opening to expose the drowned sailors at the bottom of the sea. Henry Shady and the murdering wheels of Morgan's car, Tom Cobb and the candy wrappers in the wastebasket, Jeffery Peck and the letter that summoned him to his death, Arlo Field and the whetstone that sharpened Morgan's sword.

"Mrs. Bailey?"

Sarah was afraid. She put her hand on her belly and begged her son, her daughter, to help her now, but the baby lay still. Carefully she put down the phone and turned around. "Morgan, I have to go now."

Morgan dropped the other phone, letting it dangle on its rubber cord and bump against the wall. He had barely heard the voice of Sergeant Hasty. He had not been paying attention. He smiled at Sarah, because at last he had un-

covered the core of his torment, and it was a blessed discovery. There would never be any end to the marauders,
that was what he knew now—never in all future time.
Only when there was nothing to take from him, nothing
to deprive him of, would he be at rest. "All right, then," he
said, "go." He was making a strange noise in his throat.

Hastily Sarah snatched up her bag. With a farewell
glance at Morgan, she opened the door, hurried down the
stairs, and slipped out into the night.

Behind her, moving swiftly half a block behind, Morgan
stalked her, hissing, stretching out his neck, arching his
powerful wings.

᙭   *CHAPTER 40*   ᙭

KING. Hello! Hello! What's the matter here?
CLOWN. A man dead!
KING. I fear you have killed him.
CLOWN. No! He has nearly killed me!
                    Traditional British Mummers' Play

In obedience to the command of Arlo Field, croaked at her from his hospital bed, Chickie Pickett called Homer Kelly and told him about the two men in the foreground of Arlo's picture of the forty-four suns in the sky. "It's Jeffery Peck, all right," said Chickie, "and the other guy is Morgan Bailey."

"My God, are you sure?"

"Of course I'm sure. Morgan and Sarah live upstairs from me. I see them every day."

"But that means—Jesus! Well, thank you, Ms. Pickett. That's a big help."

It was December twenty-fourth, Christmas Eve. Homer put down the phone, passed along Chickie's stunning news to Mary, and sat down to dinner—a sirloin steak, hot and rare on a heated plate, a baked potato, and a large helping of out-of-season asparagus.

Mary stared at him in horror, and threw her napkin on the table. "Morgan Bailey!" She leaped up from her chair. "But that means he's responsible for the other things too, for poisoning Tom Cobb and trying to kill Arlo Field."

"Well, maybe it does and maybe it doesn't. Hey, what are you doing? Where are you going?"

Mary hauled on her coat, snatched Homer's parka off its hooks, and dumped it in his lap. "It's Morgan's jealousy, haven't you seen it? He's obsessive about Sarah. He's dan-

229

gerous, Homer." Mary's amateur psychoanalytic diagnosis of Morgan Bailey was turning out to be right, she had been right all along. She dragged Homer out of his chair.

Homer felt like whimpering, "It's Christmas Eve," but he put on his coat and stumbled after Mary down the icy porch steps. "Where the hell do they live?"

"On Maple Avenue." Mary lunged at her car and flung open the door. "It's near Inman Square. I went there once last fall, on the bus, but we can park on the street, somewhere, anywhere, legal or illegal, who cares?"

"My wife, the notorious desperado," whined Homer, ducking in on the other side of the car and whacking his head on the roof.

Mary had never made the trip to Cambridge in less than twenty-five minutes. This time it took nineteen. "Here," she said, "this fireplug will do nicely." She swooped into a forbidden space on Cambridge Street, and turned off the engine.

"My God, woman, you're sticking out into the street."

"Oh, come on, Homer. Don't be such a fusspot."

Recklessly Mary climbed a snowbank. Homer jumped out of the car, wallowed around the fireplug, and galloped after her in the direction of Maple Avenue.

"Wait," said Homer, "isn't that—?"

Mary stopped in her tracks. "It's Sarah. And he's there too. Look, Homer, it's Morgan."

It was exactly like the first time, like the day when Mary had seen Morgan secretly following Sarah along the same sidewalk. Now Sarah was hurrying, picking her way swiftly along the path where the snow had been cleared, her footsteps loud in the deserted street, while Morgan followed silently behind her. He was walking faster, coming closer, catching up.

Homer and Mary stood behind a tall stand of bushes and watched Sarah stop on the curb to cross to the other side. She was waiting for the heavy truck that lumbered toward her, heading for Somerville.

The hair on the back of Homer's neck stood on end. "What the hell is he doing?"

Morgan was racing at his wife, his neck outstretched, a hissing sound coming from his throat, his arms spread wide, his coattails flapping. He rushed at Sarah and threw out his arms to shove her into the path of the truck. By a violent effort Homer reached her first and snatched her out of the way.

Morgan's momentum drove him forward. The driver of the truck cursed and slammed on his brakes, but he was too late. Morgan Bailey lay in the street with crushed beak and broken neck and shattered wings, his obsession dying with him, his torment at an end.

CHAPTER 41

In a manger laid and wrapped I was,
So very poor, this was my chance—
Betwixt an ox and a silly poor ass,
To call my true love to the dance.
                    Carol, "My Dancing Day"

Harvard University was still in a quandary. The death of old Maggody was the breaking point. It brought matters severely to a head. The poor old man had crept to the very door of Harvard's Vice-President for Government and Community Affairs, and in his extremity he had knocked, and he had not been let in. He had frozen to death on the doorstep only three days before Christmas. It looked bad, very bad indeed.

Worse still, one of the homeless women from Nifto's insane tent city had holed up in Henshaw's garage, hugely swollen, ready to give birth. A few hours later her child was born in Saint Elizabeth's Hospital, a howling baby boy.

It was a perfect Christmas story, full of pathos and righteous indignation. NO ROOM AT THE INN, proclaimed the *Cambridge Chronicle*. NO ROOM AT THE INN, repeated the *Boston Globe* and *The New York Times*. Gretchen's baby was famous, and the *Boston Herald* named Harvard its Scrooge of the Year.

After Christmas, the story would have died, if a single representative of the press had not gone back to Saint Elizabeth's, hoping to eke out a piece on the status of homeless single moms.

Her questions soon petered out, because Gretchen didn't think of herself as a homeless single mom. She was more like a lost princess. Her responses didn't make much sense. The woman from the *Cambridge Chronicle* put away her notebook and asked a random question. "You didn't happen to see Mr. Maggody, did you, when he dragged himself to the door of Henshaw's house?"

"Well, no," said Gretchen. "Well, like I guess I did, sort of. I saw Palmer carrying him. Well, I mean, he was carrying somebody, and I guess it was Maggody." The newswoman took her notebook out again. "Palmer? You mean Palmer Nifto? Palmer Nifto brought Maggody there? You mean Maggody was already dead, and Nifto brought him to Henshaw's front door?"

"Well, yeah, I guess so. Like, well, he was carrying him sort of over his shoulder, and then he put him down on the porch."

"You saw all this from the garage?"

"Oh, right. There's this window. You can see the front door through the window."

Gretchen had no idea she was betraying the clever manipulations of Palmer Nifto. She cuddled her homely baby and knitted him a sweater, and made up her mind not to turn him over to the Department of Social Services.

For Palmer it was a final stroke of ill luck. It had been bad enough when the uproar caused by the death of Maggody was displaced in the public mind by shock over the death of Jeffery Peck and the attack on Arlo Field. But this was worse. Now that everybody knew Palmer Nifto had picked up a corpse and moved it in order to blacken the good name of Harvard University, Maggody was back in the headlines with a vengeance, and so was Palmer Nifto. And there was an even grimmer question. What if Nifto himself had put the old man out in the snow to freeze to death? Palmer's goose was cooked.

In the highest counsels of Harvard Yard it was the juiciest bit of news, a morsel of Christmas pudding. As Palmer's stock went down, Harvard's went up.

Ellery Beaver laughed so hard he could hardly relay the news to the General Counsel on the phone. Of course the General Counsel was delighted, and so was the Dean of Faculty. They all agreed that the old man's death was a shame, but at least it had not happened on the premises of the Vice-President for Government and Community Affairs. The craven exploitation of the old man's death by Palmer Nifto made him a laughingstock. His outrageous demand for a piece of Harvard real estate lost all credibility.

On the twenty-seventh of December, while Sanders Theatre resounded with the Wednesday-afternoon performance of the Christmas Revels, the Dean and the General Counsel and Ellery Beaver met for a late lunch in the Faculty Club to consider their options.

"We simply ignore Nifto," said Ellery.

"Exactly," agreed the Dean. "We don't have to dignify the man with seminars and teach-ins and all that sort of thing."

"And we certainly don't transfer any Harvard real estate," said the General Counsel. "After all, Nifto has put himself completely out of the picture."

The General Counsel leaned forward with a shrewd suggestion. "Here's my idea. We negotiate through a third party, not with Nifto. Some highly respected and impeccable person *outside* the university chooses a charitable agency to which the university would then contribute funds."

"An *already existing* agency," suggested the Dean of Faculty, nodding and smiling. The Dean was a humane man

who contributed privately to a number of charitable organizations, and he had names on the tip of his tongue. "The Greater Boston Food Bank, the Massachusetts Coalition for the Homeless, Shelter Incorporated? Something of that sort?"

"The charm of it is," said the General Counsel, "we simply ignore Nifto. He'll be left high and dry."

They finished their coffee and gathered up their coats. As they moved toward the door, the Dean of Faculty murmured in Ellery Beaver's ear, "What exactly is the state of your chief?"

"I'm afraid I don't know," said Ellery, his voice deepening with sorrow. "He hasn't shown up in the office since Nifto dropped the old codger on his doorstep. I don't know what the hell's going on."

⚙ *CHAPTER 42* ⚙

Ye winged seraphs, fly! Bear the news!
Ye winged seraphs, fly, like comets through the sky,
Fill vast eternity with the news, with the news,
Fill vast eternity with the news!
American folk hymn, "Wondrous Love"

G retchen Milligan's baby was five days old when the supernova in the constellation Sagittarius was discovered, like an outrageously exaggerated star of Bethlehem.

It was Arlo Field's discovery. Of course, Arlo didn't know a supernova was waiting for him when he argued his way out of the hospital and walked straight down Cambridge Street to the Science Center and took the elevator to the astronomy lab on the eighth floor.

He felt fine. There was a thick bandage on his neck, and he had a bunch of pills to take, but he felt strong enough to work. He wanted to get on with his studies of reversing solar oscillations before he was fired.

And he wanted to see Sarah. He was confused about Sarah. Her husband was dead, he knew that, and it had been Morgan's sword that had landed Arlo in the hospital. And Morgan was responsible for the deaths of all those other guys. What did it mean for Sarah? Was she all right? She had not come to see him in the hospital, not once. Not even once.

"Well, look who's here," said Harley Finch. "For a while we thought you were a goner."

"What's up?" murmured Arlo, leaning over the solar image on the observation table, watching the slow change of the granular surface, inspecting the latest crop of sunspots foreshortened on the eastern limb.

"Chairman wants to see you whenever you can make it."

"He does, does he?" breathed Arlo. "I can't guess why."

Harley grinned. "Sorry, Arlo."

Oh, well, he'd known it was coming. Arlo put his finger on a bright speck near the western limb of the sun. What was that? The sun was hot and fiery, but it didn't give off sparks. Could it be a planet, Venus or Jupiter, there on the path of the ecliptic, right next to the sun? He had never observed a planet so near the sun, not even with more powerful instruments.

His heart quickened. Turning, he snatched the *Nautical Almanac* off the shelf.

"What are you doing?" Harley Finch came closer and looked inquisitively at the solar image.

Oh, no, you don't, you bastard. That star is mine.

Harley saw nothing. He looked blankly at the observing table, then drifted away and turned over his papers, keeping a cautious eye on Arlo.

No, the bright speck wasn't the planet Venus. Venus was in Capricorn. And it wasn't Jupiter either, because the sun had already passed Jupiter earlier in December. Saturn was out of the question too, moseying along through Aquarius.

Arlo went back to the observing table and looked again, fearful that the little spark would have disappeared, that it was some momentary anomaly. But it was still there, brighter than ever. It must be, it had to be, what else could it be but a nova, a supernova, a tremendously bright supernova, visible in the daytime smack up against the sun?

He didn't want to make his phone call with Harley listening. Somehow Harley would horn in, claim credit, say, Oh, yes, I saw that before you came in.

Arlo ambled out into the hall, shut the door, ran to the elevator, pressed the button, and waited in a fever of impatience. Suppose some other solar astronomer was already announcing the discovery of a supernova at right ascension eighteen hours, twenty-eight minutes, declination minus twenty-three degrees, thirty-two minutes? There must be hundreds of optical devices of one kind or another aimed at the sun right now on the daylight side of the planet.

The elevator arrived. Arlo dodged in and dropped to the ground floor, laughing at his own greed for recognition. But the supernova was his, damnit, it was all his.

Thank God, one of the public phones was free. Arlo dialed the number of the Central Bureau for Astronomical Telegrams with a trembling finger, muffed it, dialed again. "Hello, Johnny, has anybody reported a supernova?"

"Not lately. Is this Arlo? Aren't you supposed to be in the hospital? But, hey, that's great. Why didn't you call it in right away? I've been here all night."

"Because I only just found it—just now, in broad daylight—that's why. I mean, this must be some spectacular nova. It's right up against the sun."

"God, Arlo, are you sure it's not a mistake? Some kind of drug you're taking? Because, Jesus, it would be the brightest goddamn nova in history. Oh, you bet, I'll phone Kitt Peak. Got to have confirmation before I tell everybody else. My God, Arlo, visible in the daytime! I hope to hell you're right. We'll both look like damn fools if it's just some fluke."

Arlo hung up. His stitches hurt and he wanted to lie down, but he was overjoyed.

Before the day was out, his supernova was confirmed by the solar astronomers at Kitt Peak, and the news was flashed all over the world. His exploding star in the constellation Sagittarius was the brightest in recorded history. It was bright because it was near, only six hundred light-years away, within the galaxy, close enough to escape being veiled by interstellar gas and dust. It was brighter than Tycho's supernova, brighter than Kepler's, brighter than Supernova 1987A in the Large Magellanic Cloud. It might even be as bright as the exploding star Geminge, whose remnants enclosed the solar system, the supernova that must have astonished the Neanderthals. For a week or ten days before Arlo's star began to fade, it was brighter than the planet Venus.

Astronomers all over the world turned away from whatever they were doing to look at it. The shutters of observatory domes on a Chilean mountaintop rolled back, they rumbled open in Japan and Arizona and Switzerland and South Africa. NASA astronomers in Florida abandoned the regular schedule for their satellite and aimed it at the newly exploded star, and so did the men and women guiding the Hubble telescope poised seven miles above the earth. The Very Large Array in New Mexico aimed its twenty-seven dishes at Arlo's star. The X-ray satellite Rosat examined it too, from the emptiness of outer space. The rapidly changing spectrum, with its extraordinary alternation of dark and bright lines, was recorded by excited observers everywhere.

Since the supernova was discovered not long after Christmas, the *Boston Herald* proclaimed on page 1—

ASTRONOMER DISCOVERS CHRISTMAS STAR

Another *Herald* editor had a mawkish stroke of genius. Remembering the story about Gretchen Milligan's baby, NO ROOM AT THE INN, he combined it with the one about the star with stunning effect—

CHRISTMAS STAR SHINES ON HOMELESS CHILD

Arlo saw the *Herald* that day and thought sardonically that if the star had anything at all to proclaim it would be about some event 170,000 years ago, when the explosion had actually happened. And the burst of neutrinos shooting out of the star's surface would certainly have destroyed whatever life forms existed on its own planets, if there were any, frying everything, including any infant saviors who might happen to have been lying in Sagittarian mangers.

Chickie Pickett was thrilled about the supernova. "Golly, Arlo," she said, "will they name it after you?"

"Oh, no. It's just Supernova 1995K." But Arlo knew with a warm sense of vainglory that his name would always be linked with the brightest supernova in history. People were already calling it Field's Star.

The director of the observatory called him in and congratulated him.

"I understand you should have been in bed, you idiot," he said, beaming. "But thank God you weren't. Nobody else might have noticed the thing until it had gone halfway through its cycle, and that would have been a terrible loss. Oh, by the way, we're about to appoint an associate professor in stellar photometry. Are you interested? Oh, I know you've been working on solar stuff, but the sun is a star, after all."

"But I thought Harley was in line for that job," said Arlo innocently.

"Harley?" The director seemed puzzled. "Oh, you mean Harley Finch? I—uh—think he's accepted a position at the university in Pancake Flat, Arizona."

PART SEVEN

THE WOOING

Madame, I have come to court you,
If your favor I should win.
If you make me kindly welcome,
Then perhaps I'll come again.

Madame, I have rings and jewels,
Madame, I have house and land.
Madame, I've a world of treasure,
If you'll be at my command.

What care I for your world of jewels⸮
What care I for your house and land⸮
What care I for your world of treasure⸮
All I want is a handsome man.

Saint George and the Dragon

CHAPTER 43

O then bespoke the baby
Within his mother's womb—
"Bow down then the tallest tree
For my mother to have some."

Then bowed down the highest tree,
Unto his mother's hand
Then she cried, "See, Joseph,
I have cherries at command."

O eat your cherries, Mary,
O eat your cherries now,
O eat your cherries, Mary,
That grow upon the bough!

"The Cherry Tree Carol"

Sarah Bailey had suffered terrible things. She had loved her husband and feared him, he had tried to kill her and then had killed himself instead, and her baby was frozen inside her. But Sarah carried on as usual in a trance of coolness and calmness. Under her guidance the Revels went on and on, one perfect performance after another.

There were six between Christmas and the New Year. The Morris men danced; Saint George fell dead and was revived again in the person of Walt, the Old Master. The children skipped and chirped, the cherry tree bowed down to Mary, the chorus sang and danced, the dragon raked the air with his claws, Homer Kelly was sometimes Father Christmas and sometimes the fierce giant, and the Abbots Bromley horn dancers paced in and out, weaving their mysterious patterns on the darkened stage.

Sanders Theatre was as packed as ever. Enraptured people filled all the benches, basking in the glow from the stage, and at intermission they trailed after the performers into the high corridor and danced in a giant spiral, singing about the lord of the dance. Some danced in rhythm and some fell over their own feet, but they all bobbed up and down, working their way into the middle of the spiral and out again, until the music stopped and they found their way back to their seats.

Sarah didn't dance. She was stiff and cold in head and body. Her child too was stiff and cold, rigidly asleep in some sort of fetal coma—dead perhaps, most probably dead. When the Revels were all over she would see the doctor again, but she knew what he would tell her. He would listen for the baby's heartbeat and then say solemnly, "I'm sorry, Mrs. Bailey."

But when Arlo Field came back to the Revels to take the part of Saint George in the last performance of the season, Sarah felt warmth flush her cheeks and spread along her arms and legs. She sat in the front row and watched the sword dancers cut him down, and the Fool revive him with a sprig of holly. She beamed at Arlo as he sprang up and pronounced himself cured—

> *Good morning, gentlemen,*
> *a-sleeping I have been.*
> *I've had such a sleep*
> *as the like was never seen.*

He looked gravely down at Sarah as he sang, and the ardor of his look flooded through her, turning keys and loosening locks all over her body. When it was time for intermission and Arlo danced off the stage and took her hand, leading the procession into the hall, he murmured, "It's already three minutes longer."

"What is?" said Sarah, smiling at him, although she didn't care, it didn't matter what he meant. She was hardly aware of her dancing feet. The people surging past her were a grinning blur. She saw only Arlo's face, looking at her so kindly.

"The sunlight, it lasts three minutes longer than on the shortest day. The sun has started to come back."

"Oh, yes, I'm glad." And then the warmth sank deep into Sarah, and she felt something move inside her. Her child was awake, it was alive. Her baby too was dancing.

CHAPTER 44

Then afterwards baptized I was,
The Holy Ghost on me did glance.
My Father's voice heard from above,
To call my true love to the dance.
                        Carol, "My Dancing Day"

"Well, how about it, Homer? Aren't you going to tell me I was right?"

"Right? What about?"

"Right about Morgan Bailey. Right about the goose when Henry Shady was killed. Right about Morgan's obsessional jealousy."

Homer had to admit it. He apologized handsomely for having disbelieved in the goose, and for not having recognized the menace of Morgan Bailey. He was abject and humble. "It's true," he said sheepishly, "I was a rotten observer. I didn't understand what was happening. You tried to tell me, and I wouldn't listen."

Mary laughed. She felt justified at last. The seesaw of her marriage, out of balance for so long, with Homer at the heavy end and Mary herself dangling sky-high, was dead-level once again.

In triumph she exacted an act of atonement. "I'm going to the baptism," she said, "and you're going with me."

"Baptism! Whose baptism?"

"Gretchen Milligan's baby's."

"Oh, Lord, have I got to?"

"Yes, Homer, you've got to."

Of course it turned out to be a highly sentimental occasion. Everybody from Harvard Towers was there, sitting in the white pews in the Unitarian church in Harvard Square. Also present were the counselors and pregnant girls from Bright Day in Somerville, and the loyal kids from Phillips Brooks House and the staff people from the shelter at First Church Congregational and all the First Church women who had done such a lot of cooking on a large scale. Palmer Nifto was there too, making his last public appearance.

Gretchen had chosen a name from the British royal family. She beamed as the minister baptized her baby with water from the baptismal bowl.

"That bowl is famous," whispered Mary to Homer. "It's really old. They have to bring it over from the Boston Museum of Fine Arts whenever there's a christening."

"No kidding." Homer winced as little Andrew Windsor Milligan threw back his head and howled.

Afterward everyone milled around and said hello to everybody else. Palmer Nifto kissed Gretchen and congrat-

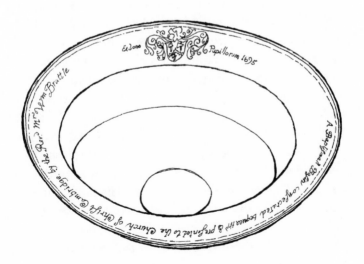

ulated her, without uttering a word about her betrayal. He took his revenge on the world in another way.

"Okay," said the deliveryman from the Boston Museum, "you're through with the christening bowl, right? I'll take it back. Where is it?"

"Well, it was right here on this table a moment ago," said the dumbfounded clergyman.

"I saw it there myself," said Mary Kelly. "Where can it be?"

"Listen, they'll skin me alive at the museum. That's a very valuable piece of seventeenth-century silver. What the hell did you do with it?"

They turned the church upside down, but the 250-year-old Dummer Christening Bowl was nowhere to be found.

Palmer Nifto too disappeared from the face of the earth. He was not seen again at Harvard Towers. And without his direction, sporadic and zigzagging though it had been, the tent city came apart.

On the first day of the new year there was another severe snowstorm, turning to sleet and rain. Next morning the tents began coming down. Mary and Homer Kelly slipped and splashed from tent to tent, helping to roll up sleeping bags and dismantle the command tent and dispose of miscellaneous baggage and say goodbye.

The homeless people of Harvard Towers were still homeless.

Why had the protest failed? Mary suspected a lack of the right kind of leadership. Oh, Palmer Nifto had been clever all right. He had checkmated every move of the police and the university, time after time. His fault had been a failure of sympathy with the very people he was trying to help.

The truth was, there was no heart in Palmer Nifto. The

terrible problems of the people who had entrusted themselves to his care—old Guthrie with his senility, Gretchen
with her teeming fertility, Maggody with his helplessness,
Bob Chumley with his cocaine addiction, and bossy Emily
Pollock—to Palmer they were merely cards in a hand of
poker. The people he called the establishment had won
because they sensed this fact about him.

If Palmer had been a different kind of leader, an idealist,
no matter how foolish and wrongheaded, he might have
been unconquerable. The lords of the earth could not have
ignored a worthy cause in combination with honest saint-
liness. But a crusade led by a scheming tactician was an
easy target.

They simply finessed Palmer Nifto.

Ellery Beaver and the Dean of Faculty peered through the
tracery of the wrought-iron gate that was the gift of the
class of 1879 and watched the tent city come down. "It's
sad," said the Dean of Faculty. "You have to admit, it's a
little sad."

They stared at Emily Pollock as she struggled with her
grocery cart, trying to push it through the slush on its little
wheels. The snow was filthy, covered with black specks.
The edges of the grubby heaps mounded beside the brick
walkway had been trampled into dark plates like sheet
metal.

"Of course it's sad," said Ellery Beaver. "God knows, it's
sad. But you have to agree, this isn't the way to fix the situation. Protests and demands, you can't cure the homeless
problem that way. It's all wrong. It's got to be solved ra-
tionally by people of intelligence and goodwill and every
sort of expertise. They've got to sit down together and
penetrate into the very heart of things." Ellery waved his

hands right and left, as though the bright cold air around him were peopled by men and women of godlike wisdom and compassion. He had a vision of noble figures in Grecian robes sitting on the steps of Memorial Church, counseling together.

"Intelligence and goodwill, that's right," repeated the Dean of Faculty. "Expertise, exactly, that's all it would take." He glanced sideways at Ellery Beaver. "Speaking of intelligence, what's the latest scoop on your boss? He's better, I hope?"

"Alas, no." Ellery turned away with the Dean and they started back across the Yard. "He still hasn't shown up in the office. I don't know what the hell's going on. The man needs psychiatric evaluation, that's for sure. Sticky wicket."

But as they parted company in Harvard Yard, Ernest Henshaw was at last ready to leave his house on Berkeley Street.

"Ernest, you're driving me crazy," said his wife, "standing around mooning like that. Why don't you go for a walk? Get out of the house into the fresh air? It would do you a world of good."

"Yes," said Henshaw, brightening, as an idea occurred to him. He put on his coat and scarf and gloves and pulled on his galoshes, and walked straight out of the house. Helen Henshaw sighed with relief.

Walking in a dream, Henshaw headed for Harvard Square, looking neither left nor right.

The square was crowded, as usual, with a flood of people on their way somewhere, crossing the intersection to the kiosk in the middle of the street, standing on the curb and crossing again to the other side, emerging from the subway and flowing along the sidewalk past the Harvard Coop and the bank, heading for JFK Street.

It wasn't the people in motion who interested Henshaw. It was the still ones, the unmoving ones, the people sitting on the sidewalk or leaning against the iron fence beside the cemetery, or sitting on wooden benches smoking cigarettes.

To Henshaw they looked wonderful. They glowed with an adorable simplicity. No multiplying heaps of boxes were piled up beside them. They did not own half a million separate and individual objects. They were alone, they were themselves, they were nothing but themselves.

Twice he walked past a grim-looking old man with the stub of a cigarette between forefinger and thumb. He walked past him a third time, staring at him. The man avoided his gaze, lost in his own emptiness, his own lack of boxes, his pure isolation from tens of thousands of miscellaneous possessions.

Henshaw did not speak to him. Walking past for the fourth time, he slowed his steps, turned to the fence, walked up to it, turned his back to it, and leaned his Harris tweed coat against it.

Then—very slowly—he slid down until he was sitting on the sidewalk. It was amazingly comfortable. Henshaw pulled at his pants, hunched up his legs, and slumped forward.

The man beside him did not look up.

PART EIGHT

THE LUCK

Be there loaf in your locker
and sheep in your fold,
A fire on the hearth
and good luck in your lot,
Money in your pocket
and a pudding in the pot.
Saint George and the Dragon

CHAPTER 45

Bells in the cold tower, 'midst the snow of winter,
Sound out the Spring song,
That we may remember
Bells in the cold tower, after the long snowing
Come months of growing.

Traditional Hungarian carol

The sun was low in the sky, moving toward the horizon in a long shallow arc. Slanting rays touched the old tombstones in the ancient churchyard near Harvard Square, grazed the thin hair on Henshaw's head, skipped across Massachusetts Avenue to Harvard Yard, struck the gold pennant on the steeple of Memorial Church, and glowed on the red-tile roof of Sever Hall.

It was four o'clock. The bell in the steeple of Memorial Church clanged for sixty seconds to mark the hour. Within the hundred buildings scattered around the Yard and along Oxford Street and Kirkland, Francis Avenue and Divinity, scores of men and women labored, free for the moment from the task of lecturing to classrooms full of students. In a hundred scholarly disciplines they bowed over books or crouched in front of computer monitors, exploring their individual jeweled caves.

On the eighth floor of the Science Center, Arlo Field gazed at the solar image cast by the spectrohelioscope on the observing table. In the last week the sun had moved away from Supernova 1995K, and therefore there was no bright speck beside it. Astronomers everywhere were monitoring from hour to hour the extraordinary changes in the optical and radio emissions of Field's Star, but here in Arlo's teaching lab there was only the sun, this middle-range ordinary star, dependable and stable, replacing the lost energy of its shining by nuclear fusion deep within its core. It was not about to blow up.

The tremendous heat of the interior was not visible in this light, nor the spicules and flares thrown up from gigantic electromagnetic storms. It was strange, thought Arlo, how innocent the sun looked when you saw it in the sky, that friendly and necessary companion glowing through the branches of trees, sending down its basking heat—and how alarming it was really, enlarged in an X-ray image with all the wild splendor of its coronal holes.

Arlo shrugged himself into his coat and went out on the terrace. As usual, the universe expanded around him in all directions. Most of it was invisible at the moment, but it was there all the same. His childhood cosmos was still part of it, the far-flung planets rolling around the sun, the Milky Way arching overhead, and the Orion nebula flinging out its veils of gauze. Now his vision stretched to the vast cluster of galaxies within the constellation Hydra, to quasars emitting more energy than the Milky Way, to black holes warping space and time, to the fringe of galaxies on the edges of the perceivable universe.

Looking over the railing on the south side of the terrace, he could see the overpass with its half-dismantled campsite, and a number of little figures pulling down the remaining tents and walking away, their problems still unsolved. A woman in a purple hat was doing something strange, but he couldn't see what it was.

From here they all looked very small. The earth itself was small, with its squirming surface of organic life, all those struggling creatures taking themselves so seriously, as if it mattered what happened on this small piece of rock wobbling around a minor star so undistinguished that it was right in the middle of the main stellar sequence. These hectic lives, these squabbling nations, these tiny destinies working themselves out on this microscopic planet, how could they matter in a universe so complex and so vast? Once again he asked himself which was the more real, the more important.

Arlo watched one of the homeless women trying to push a grocery cart over the rough snow, and told himself that misery was important. Surely it was at least as important as the explosion of Supernova 1995K; in fact, it stank to high heaven. Then he looked east in the direction of Maple Avenue, where he had just left Sarah sleeping, drowsy and smiling, content with the drumming inside her, the lively motions of the child that was to be born in April. Love too was important, as important as the black hole in Cygnus X-1 or the Cepheid variables in the Magellanic Clouds.

Down on the overpass, Dr. Box ignored the departing residents of Harvard Towers and the people passing between the Science Center and the Yard. She had an agenda of her own. She was delaying the sunset, holding it back by a method employed by the wizards of New Caledonia. Scraping a few inches of the walk clear of snow with her shoe, she put down a bundle of well-chosen charms, struck a match, and set the bundle on fire. As a wisp of smoke rose into the cold air, she invoked her ancestors in Cornish, New Hampshire, and addressed the western horizon. "Sun! I do this that you may be burning hot and eat up all the clouds in the sky."

From his high vantage point at the railing of the balcony on the eighth floor of the Science Center, Arlo had forgotten the woman in the purple hat. He was watching the winter sun go down over the Charles River and Harvard

Stadium and the cities of Allston and Brighton. It was taking too long. Feeling the cold, he went inside and closed the door. He could keep track of the sunset on the observation table. There now, at last the image was flattening and trembling at the edges. As he watched, it grew faint and fainter, then darkened and disappeared.

Arlo looked at his wristwatch and smiled. It must be running a little fast. It said four-twenty-four, as though the sun were setting even later than the almanac's prediction. But of course his watch was wrong in the right direction. The lengthening of the hours of sunlight was inexorable. Once again the Northern Hemisphere had passed through the shortest day. The earth was roving closer and closer to the vernal equinox, spinning and turning without end.

Spring would come. There was no way of stopping it. The dance would go on.

> *Our play is done; we must be gone.*
> *We stay no longer here.*
> *We wish you all, both great and small,*
> *A happy, bright New Year!*
> Saint George and the Dragon

⌘ *AFTERWORD* ⌘

The performance of the Revels in this work of fiction is modeled after the Christmas Revels celebrated each year at Sanders Theatre in Cambridge, Massachusetts. The gifted creators of that annual festival of course know a different and deeper Revels, and so do the hundreds of volunteer participants. My outsider's interpretation is not the fault of the generous people who answered my questions.

A principal sourcebook for this story was John Langstaff's *Saint George and the Dragon: A Mummer's Play.* Another was *The Christmas Revels Songbook*, compiled by Nancy and John Langstaff. Many carol verses were taken from *The Oxford Book of Carols.*

With her kind permission the title of this book comes from Susan Cooper's poem, "The Shortest Day." I have also used passages from her dramatized version of "Sir Gawain and the Green Knight," as well as her words for the song about the donkey, "Orientis Partibus," and the carol "Sing We Noël."

A number of the chapter epigraphs are taken from Alex Helm's book, *The English Mummers' Play*, which gives verbatim many similar local versions of a few traditional original types.

Astronomer Alan Hirshfeld of the University of Massachusetts introduced me to the mysteries of the analemma, and figured out the coordinates of the supernova. I had friendly help, too, from Harvard astronomers Robert Kirshner, Josh Grindlay, and Robert Noyes.

Tremendous thanks are due also to the Reverend Stewart Guernsey, that witty and compassionate friend of the homeless.

The view given here of Memorial Hall is the last glimpse of an old friend. The interior is currently being rehabilitated to serve Harvard students in new ways. In an earlier novel I high-handedly restored the pyramidal roof of the tower, which had been destroyed by fire in 1956. The actual living tower has remained ever since uncrowned, unpinnacled, and unclocked, a sad stump rising on the Cambridge horizon. There are rumors—whispered, fading, whispered again—that the tall summit is to rise once more, with or without its fabled clocks and pinnacles.